Jaina

LORENDA'S GAMBLE

It was a pleasure to get to know you a bit.

Hope you enjoy the read and let me know what you thought of it when you're done!

By

Craig Harriman

charriman427@gmail.com

Copyright © 2023, Craig Harriman
First Edition

Without limiting the rights under copyright reserved above,
no part of this publication may be reproduced,
stored in or introduced into a retrieval system,
or transmitted, in any form or by any means
(electronic, mechanical, photocopying, recording, or otherwise),
without the prior written permission of the copyright owner of this book.

Published by Aventine Press
55 East Emerson St.
Chula Vista CA, 91911
www.aventinepress.com

ISBN: 978-1-955162-22-7

ALL RIGHTS RESERVED

Acknowledgements

Thanks to those who have critiqued this novel for your time, interest and suggestions. All errors in this book are mine and mine alone. All characters in this book are fictional.

DEDICATION

This book is dedicated to Linda, and our grandchildren: Jaden, Dylan, Aschim, Katiana, Keb, Beatrice, and Fiona.

And special thanks to Carol Hazelwood (author), who helped get this book published.

Chapter One
A Decision

David woke up at 6:30. It was his usual time. Lorenda, his wife rolled over, still asleep. He got out of bed and quietly walked over to the bathroom, leaving the lights out, so as not to disturb her. He could hear her lightly snoring as he shaved. While he was showering, he thought how every day was the same. The hot water felt good cascading down his body. The steam rising as he sucked it in.

Day after day, week after week and year after year, the same routine. He felt sad this morning, defeated. He and Lorenda had not been getting along for a long time. Their marriage was great in the early years, but gradually they had lost interest in each other. He didn't know how to change it. Sex was almost non-existent. He had made an effort to get along better a few times, but in the last couple years, he had just given up. It wasn't worth the effort. Oddly, he was not interested in any other women. He and Lorenda co-existed, but that was about the extent of it. For now, he would just let it ride, but he knew eventually, he would want a divorce. He felt he really needed a change.

He got out of the shower and grabbed a towel. His clothes hung neatly in the closet, cleaned and pressed. He dressed casually, but for success. It was important to him to make a good impression on customers and staff.

At breakfast, he had cereal and toast. That was the first time that he didn't have bacon and eggs for years. Well, that was a change. He liked it. He read the paper as he sipped his second cup of coffee. There was some kind of a virus coming out of China that the health officials seemed to be quite concerned about. Another chicken flu or something. Outside, the wind was whipping the snow crystals on the kitchen windowpane. Jesus it was cold for this time of year.

7:35 He hit the remote control to start his Jeep Cherokee and opened the garage door to let out the exhaust fumes. He had been buying Jeeps now for about ten years. A new one every two years. He hated repairing anything, especially vehicles and the auto dealers charged outrageous hourly rates. $140.00 per hour for labor. That's insane he thought. It amazed him that people went to dealerships. They just got ripped off and never mind those extended warranties.

His street was icy and full of ruts. You never see a snowplow down here he thought. What the fuck does the city of Saskatoon do with our tax dollars? He arrived at the shop at 7:55. Smith's Lock and Key opened at 8:30 and he always put the coffee on and looked over the previous day's invoices and the bank deposit before any of his staff arrived. He trusted Greg, his manager, but it always made him feel better to check over the invoices to see that everything had been charged out correctly. No mistakes made. He had to keep these guys on their toes. He had been running the locksmith shop now for nearly 23 years. It had pretty humble beginnings. He had put in long hours for the first five or six years. Once or twice he nearly threw in the towel. Gradually the business grew, and he hired more staff, bought more equipment, expanded to a bigger building. By the time he hit the ten-year mark, he was doing very well. He quit renting and bought his own building in a busy downtown location. That was a turning point. More money was accumulating in his account.

By 2020, he was set. He really didn't have to work anymore and this morning as he sat in his office pouring his third cup of coffee, he wondered why he still was. He ran his fingers through his hair and rubbed the back of his head. Over the years, David became more confident. He looked the part of a successful businessman. He stood 6 ft. 2 inches, weighed one – ninety- five. Most people thought he was handsome. At 48, he still had a full head of dark brown hair. David didn't work out, but he wasn't soft or overweight.

Yes, a change was in order. He started to brainstorm about a holiday.

Chapter Two
Another decision

Back at home, Lorenda lay in her bed, snuggled in and toasty warm under the covers. She lay there for almost twenty minutes after waking before she decided to throw back the quilt and face the day. Her marriage of 26 years was heading for the ditch and it was getting to be a struggle to be in the same house as her husband. They were both feeling miserable.

Lorenda had been unhappy for many years now. She was an attractive woman, but her husband seemed as if he wasn't interested in what she had to offer. She had been going through a severe depression. At one time, Lorenda was hearing voices in her head and felt that David was out to harm her. David and her sons had persuaded her to seek help with a phycologist. In time and with medication they got things under control. Now again, she had the feeling that David was plotting to get rid of her. No way she was going to tell anyone about this. Nobody seemed to understand what she was going through.

She crossed the room and stood by the mirror. She looked out to see if Ryan across the street was looking out his window. He was. He always was. She slowly took off her pajamas and stood in front of the mirror naked. It was a morning ritual that she never missed. Lorenda wondered if she was still as attractive to men as she once had been. Ryan didn't go to work before 9. She had no idea what he did for a living and had only met Ryan and his wife Sarah a couple times briefly. They were not friends and didn't socialize even though they lived across the street from each other. Ryan and his wife were roughly the same age as David and Lorenda. Lorenda stood there for about a minute running her hand over her tummy and down between her legs. She was a good- looking woman, 5 ft 10 inches, 145 pounds. The curves in all the right places. She had firm ample breasts, jet black hair. Lorenda pretended to look out at the snow swirling outside her second storey window. She could see Ryan peeking through his curtains. She had no desire to cheat on David, especially with Ryan, even though their marriage certainly had become cold and quite uncomfortable.

Lorenda showered, dressed and did her make up. She went downstairs and made herself some breakfast, cereal and fruit. Oranges were here favorite. She and David only ate breakfast together on Sunday, when his shop wasn't open. She had gone to half time this last year at the Safeway where she worked and next summer she would retire altogether. She didn't really like her job, but it wasn't stressful, and the pay was decent. She really had no formal training. Actually, she never even finished high school. Most of her life she had worked at lower paying jobs. David was the main breadwinner. When the boys were small, she had stayed at home. Once they started school, she found a job driving school bus. After that she worked in retail as a cashier. Lorenda had no idea what she would like to do once she did retire, but she was feeling that her life was at a standstill. There was no romance left in her marriage with David. It was over but she didn't know how to leave. They were courteous to one another, but the love and the excitement had left years ago. She really was just going through the motions lately. Nothing gave her any satisfaction. The day to day with David was monotonous and at times almost unbearable. She was always on edge and they rarely agreed on anything. She had even fantasized how she might get rid of him. Something like that was not in the realm of something she could do, but that didn't stop her from thinking about it. Lorenda's parents Miguel and Grace had been married for 49 years now. They had always gotten along well, and they raised her to be a good catholic. She just couldn't see how she could leave David.

Divorce for her meant failure and it would disappoint everyone in the family. What worried her the most was her life would change drastically. Even if David paid her alimony, she probably wouldn't be able to keep the house. She thought it would be impossible to maintain the lifestyle she now enjoyed. No doubt, the house would be sold, and she would have to rent somewhere to live. There would be loads of money wasted on lawyers. There was no way she would qualify for a mortgage on her wages. If David was out of the picture, she could keep the house, sell the business and do whatever she liked into her retirement. In addition, the voice in her head, that she thought was God, was telling her that maybe she should get rid of David before he got rid of her. Yes, she was hearing voices again. It was God. She was hearing these voices about five years ago when she was stressed out. Now the voices were back.

Both she and David were very private. They never aired their dirty laundry and as a result friends never knew that their marriage was on the rocks. Lorenda lived for her boys and the grandchildren. They had two boys Rick and Harley. Both were married and both had 2 children. Her free time was spent with her girlfriends and they often drank too much when they got together. Her drink of choice was gin.

It was Saturday and she didn't have to work, so she phoned Harley's to see if she could stop by for coffee. His wife Janice answered the phone. Janice was pleasant enough, but Lorenda never did get along with her all that well. She felt that Janice was judgemental. Janice informed her that Harley was out buying some tools but that she was welcomed to drop by. Lorenda said she would be over by 10.

The coffee was ready when Lorenda arrived. Janice still had her house coat on. She wasn't a morning person. Janice was about 40 lbs overweight, and the house was a mess as usual. This was always a thorn in Lorenda's side. If she was to admit it, Harley was kind of a mess too. Her son and his wife didn't have a great marriage either. Harley drank too much, they always had financial problems and they always seemed to have drama in their lives. Lorenda and David had bailed them out several times financially. Loans of anywhere from 2 to 15,000 dollars. Usually, half was paid back and then forgotten or written off. Janice and Harley's two boys were not very respectful. Not to David and Lorenda or anyone else for that matter. Tim and Tony were seven and six years old. They talked back to their parents, were messy like their parents, were always pretty noisy and spoiled. Lorenda loved them anyway. Janice shooed them outside when Lorenda arrived.

Over coffee today Janice was telling Lorenda that she thought Harley might be gambling again. The reason she suspected this was that most of the utility bills had gone unpaid for the last two months. Harley had gotten some counselling for his addiction, but it hadn't helped much. Janice was saying

"Harley went to play hockey last night, the game started at nine. I know all the boys stay for a couple beers after the game and to shoot the shit in the dressing room; but Harley didn't get home till after two. I'm sure he was at the casino."

Just as Janice was revealing this news, Harley got home from shopping. His mother didn't confront him with this new news because the boys were around. She would bring it up later when there was just the two of them. Janice hadn't confronted him because their relationship was already strained, and she didn't want to add fuel to the fire. Lorenda made small talk with Harley for a few minutes and then left. This was a shit show that she didn't feel like dealing with today. Not a good start to her day.

All this bullshit upset Lorenda, and she decided it was time to change her life. She had to take control and change this dead-end fucking relationship with David. That prick was cheap. She always had to get his okay to spend money and he was a control freak. Everything had to go his way when it came to making decisions.

She drove to the library. It was time to do some research on poisons, ones that perhaps would be hard to detect in an autopsy. She decided not to take any books out. Didn't want to leave any type of a trail or evidence of what she was up to. Lorenda made her way over to a corner where no one else was sitting. She even kept her gloves on while reading through the books she had selected. She didn't think she could ever do something like poisoning David, but she thought she would do some research just the same. It was a start.

CHAPTER THREE
Preparation

Back at the shop David went over the books, looked at the new work orders and delegated the jobs to be done today. He was proud of what he had accomplished with the business and he thought it was time to treat himself to a holiday or at least some time off. His mind began to wander. One of David's favorite things was reading books on survival. He also watched all the T.V. shows that had anything to do with survival. Bear Grills, Survivor man, Alone, Dual Survivors, Naked and Afraid, Life below zero, Boundless and many others. When he was younger, he had spent a fair amount of time in the North with his brother Paul and a good friend Pete. Pete had a log cabin that he had built off the grid in the northern forest that was far from any roads or towns. To get to it in summer, you had to canoe in, or use a snowmobile in the winter. It was approximately 40 miles through the bush from the nearest gravel road and about 70 miles from the nearest little town. David thought about that cabin. It had been probably seven or eight years since he was last there hunting moose with Paul and Pete. Pete had since moved to Boston a couple years ago and he doubted anyone had been there recently. He would send off an email and ask Pete if he could use it again for a couple weeks. He thought it would be fun to use the cabin as a home base and travel on foot, north into the bush and actually test out his survival skills. David considered himself a bush man. Pretty good in the bush, but never really had to test himself in a survival situation. He would talk to Lorenda about it tonight. He thought it would be really nice to get away from her for a while anyway. They hadn't been getting along too well and a break would be good.

David talked to Lorenda about his plan to get away by himself for a couple weeks. To his surprise, she readily agreed that would be a good idea. Monday morning, he fired off an e-mail to Pete to see if it would be alright to use his cabin as a home base in the next few weeks. He started to assemble some equipment to take on his trip. He had decided to walk into the cabin as he thought the ice was maybe frozen over on the river, but not necessarily so. He didn't own a snow machine, so walking was his only option. He would drive in as far as he could and then walk the rest of the way.

Where the gravel road ended, he could make his way with his truck approximately 18 miles on a trail through the bush, cross the river on an old log bridge that he and Paul had helped construct and then continue another four miles where the bush trail ended. There he would have to leave the vehicle. From there he would have to go on foot for another eighteen miles.

He would have to take a chain saw along in the vehicle, as there were always dead trees fallen across the road. Some years were worse than others depending on storms and plow winds. The going could be very slow. That was one full day, a long day. His plan was to spend the first night in or beside the truck and he could walk in the 18 miles to the cabin the next day. It was a fair hike but if the trails weren't too grown in, there should be no problem.

The cabin sat on the bank of the Beacon River. He shouldn't have any trouble finding his way as he had been in that area and stayed in the cabin at least a half dozen times in the past, although not recently. The trails were fairly easy to follow. Once he arrived there, he had all the tools and stuff necessary to survive in the bush. The cabin had all the utensils, cooking pots, axes etc. one would need, so he would carry none of that with him. He would just take in enough food, booze and essentials to last him a couple weeks. He knew Pete always left the cabin stocked with dry goods like rice, Pasta, some canned goods etc. in case of emergency.

The backpack would be heavy enough. He had learned in the past to try to keep it to less than 25 lbs. otherwise it was tough slugging through the bush. He planned to carry in a water-resistant sleeping bag for sleeping outdoors, a light ground sheet and tarp to keep any rain or snow off. He would take his 22. He wouldn't be hunting any big game, mainly just bush chickens to supplement his food supply. He hoped there was a fishing rod at the cabin. Depending on the year, you could catch fish in the river. Sometimes they were plentiful, other years you couldn't catch shit. He thought the river still should be open. It may be freezing over at this time, but he thought it unwise to try to get there by canoe. If there were sections frozen over it would be much further and harder to get there following the river, than to go over land using the bush trails.

He went to Cabella's and purchased some waterproof matches, some Jerky and freeze dried, dehydrated meals. He didn't want to take just too much as he planned on supplementing what he ate by living off the land. He would make sure he had enough coffee, tea, bread, butter, sugar, cooking oil, eggs and a few packets of dried vegetables.

In addition to the groceries, he set aside his Buck knife, a swiss army pocketknife, some wire and light rope for building shelters. Beer was too heavy to pack in, so he purchased 2 40-ounce bottles of Rye whiskey. No mix – too bulky and heavy. He hoped there may be some canned pop in the cabin. If not, well he'd mix it with water. If he was lucky there may be a tin of iced tea in the cabin that he could use for mix. If not, he was going to be roughing it. No frills.

He set a date to leave for Nov 10th. David made arrangements at his shop, leaving his manager, Greg in charge. He told them he would be gone the whole month of November although he only planned on being away two weeks or so.

There was no cell service where he was going, so he would have to be self-sufficient. This made his challenge a little more exciting in his mind. He didn't want to scratch up his jeep going in on the narrow bush trails, so he asked his son Rick if he could borrow his old 4-wheel drive. It was about 15 years old. A Toyota Tundra. Perfect bush vehicle. Sometimes heavy snow falls made it necessary to have a 4 wheel drive up there. In addition, there was some muskeg in the area. Muskeg never really freezes up, so you don't want to get stuck in it or it can be a real challenge to get out. David had been stuck several times in that country in the muskeg. You have to have a good Jack all and an axe, or chain saw to cut brush, to get yourself out. Jack up the vehicle, put logs and tree limbs in the rut, lower the vehicle, try to move forward a few inches or feet and repeat until you are once again on firm land. It can take hours or even a full day to get out. A very dirty, muddy, exhausting, and frustrating endeavor. When you are travelling in the bush with one or two other people, it affords a certain degree of safety. When you are travelling by yourself, one must be very careful. Any minor mishap, cut, or injury can be very serious. David knew this and he would be prepared.

Chapter Four
Plans most foul

Lorenda after two weeks of combing through books in the library in her spare time, came up with a plan. She knew she didn't have the guts to kill David on her own and she was too afraid to get anyone else in on the evil deed, but maybe, just maybe, she could get David to kill himself. She couldn't believe she was actually thinking about this. It was totally not her, but the idea slowly became an obsession in her mind.

He was leaving next week on his bush adventure holiday. His survival test, as he put it. Men were weird she thought. David was prone to migraine headaches. He had been for years. He usually took extra strength Tylenol or Excedrin to combat the headaches. Her research told her that cyanide was hard to trace and very deadly. She thought if she could get her hands on some cyanide and put it in some of the pain relief capsules, it might just do the trick. If he took two capsules, it should be enough to kill him. Rat poison was another option, but he would have to ingest much more of that to kill him. She could not think of a way to get enough of it into his system without him catching on. Scratch that idea.

Her research revealed that she should be able to obtain cyanide from a chemical supply store, or maybe a high school chemistry lab. Photography shops used it, as well as Jewelers. Cyanide seemed the best to use and the one that was hardest to trace. She didn't want to go out and buy any as that could leave a trail back to her.

One of her old friends Cindy was a photographer. She had a studio right in her back yard. Cindy specialized in baby pictures, weddings, graduations and such. She also experimented with black and white photography and developed her own photos in a dark room. Saturday morning Lorenda gave her a call and asked if she could come for a glass of wine as they hadn't seen each other for a couple of months. Cindy was happy to oblige. Nothing more enjoyable to her than to drink wine and gossip incessantly. The next afternoon, Lorenda brought over 2 bottles of Pino Noir and they settled in to catch up.

They talked about their husbands and their kids. How tough it was to be a parent and a wife. Lorenda told her about David's upcoming trip, and they planned a girls night out while he would be gone. Cindy let out she thought her husband may be cheating on her, but it was just a feeling. She had no real proof. Her husband Bob was spending more and more time away from home which made Cindy suspicious that something was not quite right. Cindy was also thinking that something was not right with Lorrenda. She was avoiding eye contact and just the way she was talking gave Cindy some cause for concern. She was aware that Lorenda could be very weird and unpredictable at times, but she had seemed very stable for the last couple of years.

She remembered the time that Lorenda was really pissed off with David because he was so controlling and overbearing. Something about spending too much money on clothes. They had had a big fight over it. Lorenda was in a rage and had convinced Cindy to go away to Vegas for a weekend with her to get even. She would show that son of a bitch how to spend money. Well Cindy went with her, but they left without even telling David about going. It was a total disaster. When David found out, he was in a rage. Things between them never really got back on track after that incident.

Now Cindy wondered if Lorenda was having a mid -life crisis. She certainly seemed unhappy. She let it go. Maybe it was her imagination.

Lorenda asked to see some of Cindy's recent work and so the drinking afternoon moved to the studio in the back yard. Because there was no bathroom in the studio, when the girls had to use the bathroom, they would have to go back into the house. This gave Lorenda time to snoop through her supplies and on Cindy's second bathroom break, she found what she was looking for and pocketed it. Four hours later both women were pissed to the gills, having drank the two bottles Lorenda had brought and then to top it off, a half bottle of dry gin that Cindy got from her bar. Mission accomplished.

She stumbled down the driveway and got into the car. She had her cyanide. The trip home was a little scarry and she damaged the passenger side front wheel as she took one corner a little wide and hit a curb. She vowed to herself not to drive home again in that condition. Something she had vowed a few times before.

Next day at home, Lorenda went to the medicine cabinet and found the Excedrin. There was also a bottle of extra strength Tylenol. Since David favored the Excedrin, she would use those. She pulled apart six capsules emptying the contents into the toilet bowl. She then refilled them with the cyanide. A good place to hide the capsules would be in her jewellery box and she would place them into the bottle just before he left on his trip. She wondered if she could really go through with this scheme. She wasn't a murderer, but she did want to be rid of her husband and divorce simply wasn't an alternative. She couldn't face her kids or friends, or their parents if she divorced. She felt trapped but no one had a clue of how she was really feeling.

Lorenda had thought this thing through. There would be no real motive that would point fingers at her. She hadn't increased the life insurance policy. They had bought that several years ago. She hadn't even told any friends about how unhappy she was in her marriage. When the morning of Nov 10th came around, she would place the cyanide pills in the top of the Excedrin bottle.

Six capsules should be enough to cover the top, so any two pills he shook out would be filled with the deadly poison. She had worn gloves while handling the Excedrin bottle and capsules. She hadn't taken any books out of the library, no trace to her there. No trace of her obtaining the cyanide. No extra ordinary purchases, no fights with David in public. No extra marital affairs. No nothing. The only possible link would be if the authorities found the other four tainted capsules, but why would they ever even be looking at that. They may never find the cause of death. With any luck he would die somewhere in the bush, perhaps never be found or wild animals and birds may devour his remains before authorities located his body. If he died in Pete's cabin, it may be weeks before an autopsy would be performed. Perhaps an autopsy would never even be ordered. Perhaps it would look like a natural death, maybe a heart attack? Lorenda went over all the possible scenarios. She felt pretty confident her plan would work. With David out of the way, she would be free to sell the business and retire comfortably. She would be free to meet someone new and love again. Once she had loved David, but she thought with him, she would never feel love again.

She was heady with the thought of having David out of her life. She would be free. Perhaps she would take a trip to Paris. Plans had fallen into place very quickly and without knowing it, David had played right into her hand. She may never get an opportunity like this again. She was ready to take the gamble.

CHAPTER FIVE
Departure date

Nov 10th had arrived. David had packed his things the night before. He went over his check list: Groceries, chain saw, gas, chain oil, Buck knife, pocketknife, his 22 rifle and two boxes of fifty shells each, axe, booze, tarp, compass, clothing, sleeping bag in waterproof bag, waterproof matches, lighters, flashlight, three in one light weight cooking pots, wire, and rope. He was set.

The sky was overcast, the forecast was for snow. He was up early. David was excited and wanting to get on the road. Lorenda got up with him. She made him bacon and eggs, toast and coffee. They talked over breakfast, something they hadn't done for a long time as David always got up before her. She asked him about all the supplies he had ready at the door. He told her about each item he was taking. There was one thing she brought up that he hadn't thought of. A first aid kit. There most- likely would be one at the cabin, but he thought he should maybe take a few band aids and some pain killers. That didn't take up much room and had hardly any weight to it. He went to the bathroom medicine chest; got a half dozen band aids, a few small gauze bandages and the bottle of Excedrin capsules. He told Lorenda that he would be back no later than the 24th, but everyone at the shop was told the end of the month. That way if he was late, it would be no big deal.

He packed the supplies into the back seat of the truck and after giving Lorenda a little peck on the cheek, he was off. There was a light snow falling and the roads were a little bit slippery. A line of black clouds portends a coming storm. He calculated that he would be at his turnoff into the bush by maybe 1:30 or 2:00 P.M.

From there on in, it would be slow going. At noon he stopped at a small town called Lovely. He filled with gas, bought a six pack of beer and a submarine sandwich. He ate on the road to save time. The day was getting darker as the clouds rolled in. The snow was getting heavier and the wind was picking up, making visibility poor. He had to slow down a bit, but he cracked a beer and listened to his favorite country station. Waylon Jennings was going back to Lukenbach Texas with Willie Nelson. He knew every word. He was in a great mood and he was starting to get a little buzz on from the beer. At 2:15 he reached his turn off. It was now 14 miles to the river where he would cross on an old log bridge. He would have to have a good look at it, to make sure it could hold the trucks weight. Once across he had another four miles to the end of the trail. There he would set up camp or he could sleep in the truck and then set out on his 18-mile trek to the cabin the next morning. He cracked another beer and turned up the music. He was singing along at the top of his voice. George Strait – " All my Ex's live in Texas" He loved the old country music. This new stuff was for the birds. This was already an adventure. He was having a great time and it felt so good to get away from his work and his wife.

    It was a sand and dirt road and really pretty smooth in some places. He knew that further up; the road would deteriorate, and the ruts and muskeg holes would reduce his speed but for now he could cruise along at about 15 miles an hour. In a half hour or so he should be at the bridge. Time for a pee. He reached in the back and got out a bottle of whiskey. He had a slug and chased it with beer. This was fuckin fun. The snow was even heavier now, and he really couldn't see much, but he bounced along with reckless abandon. The trail narrowed and the tree branches were slapping against the windshield from time to time. At times he had to slow down to two or three miles an hour, and sometimes he could get going to 15 or more. The truck jumped out of a rut and veered to the right. He glanced off a tree, scraping the front fender and knocking off the passenger side mirror. Rick was going to be pissed off about that. He had to stop and cut up a tree that had fallen across the road. He got out the chainsaw and the whiskey and went to work. Because of poor visibility, he had nearly run into the tree before he got the truck stopped. It took a fair bit of time as the pieces of wood were heavy to move off the road. The afternoon was wearing on and he wanted to get to the end of the road before dark. He took another good slug of whiskey when he got back into the truck and opened the last beer. It was friggin cold out and he turned up the heater. Snowing very heavily now. He carried on with not a worry. The booze gave him a false sense of well- being. He tried to speed it up a bit as time was a wastin.

Suddenly the truck was bouncing down a steep embankment. His head banging on the roof. What the hell was going on? David's mind was racing and his heart was pounding. The truck hit the river and slowly started floating down with the current. It was sinking. Water was already gushing in and it was up to his feet on the floor. The river had not yet frozen over. The bridge must have washed out with the ice flow last spring. David had to fight back the panic and think quickly. He reached into the back and grabbed his sleeping bag that was in a waterproof bag. The water was now up to his knees. There was no time to gather anything. The water was now up to his chest. He put down his window and pushed himself, sleeping bag and arms first, into the freezing water. He gasped for air as the cold enveloped his body. When he broke the surface, he didn't know which way he was facing. David was not a good swimmer, but he put his arms around the waterproof bag and kicked his feet propelling him to the opposite shore. Lucky for David that the bag was buoyant as he didn't know how to swim. It felt like an eternity. The cold was sucking the energy out of him, but luckily the river was not too wide, perhaps a hundred and forty feet in total. His feet hit bottom and he struggled in the mud to get to the bank. Exhausted and freezing he knelt down to try to regain his breath.

Looking through the snowstorm he could not make out anything that looked like the bridge. It must have washed out. Maybe this past year or maybe even before that. No one had been here recently so there was no way to tell. David tried to think clearly but it was beginning to be difficult. He had to get out of the wind, into some kind of shelter, perhaps get into his sleeping bag. The cold and fatigue was impairing his judgement. He didn't think he had enough energy to build a fire and besides that would be extremely difficult in this wind and snow. He knew he had to do something pretty quickly as hypothermia would set in soon. His teeth were chattering uncontrollably as he set off up the bank. It was steep here, the riverbank sides washed out and there were huge crevasses and holes. Making any headway was tough. Further up the bank, the willows and grasses were thick. It was hard to see anything, especially with the heavy snow. The cold gripped his body with shivers and shakes.

He made his way slowly, trying not to panic. His instinct was to run, but he knew that would be fatal. A half hour later, nearly frozen to death, his right foot fell into a hole clean up to his balls. Oh, that hurt, and he was so cold. He didn't feel he could carry on any further. No energy left. A closer look revealed that the hole was deeper and big enough for him to crawl into. He pushed the waterproof bag ahead of himself and squirmed into the darkness. In a couple of feet, the hole opened into a larger space, almost like a small cave.

David's body was trembling and shivering involuntarily. At first just at intervals, but then continuously. The shaking was non-stop. He could not control it.

He didn't know if it was his imagination, but it felt much warmer in here than outside. He was out of the wind. Although it was dark, he felt around and found there was a bed of leaves and small branches on the floor of the hole. He crawled in a little further. The dry leaves wicked away some of the water from his clothing which were almost frozen stiff. He knew it was impossible, but it almost felt like there was a little warmth in this hole. He felt around in the dark. What was this? It felt like hair. He could not comprehend what he was feeling. Was he delusional? Now he could hear something. Something like a faint breathing. Suddenly, he knew where he was. It was most likely a bear's den. His mind raced with fear. What if the bear woke up? What a way to die. Mauled by a bear in a den. He tried to stay perfectly still but couldn't stop shivering. He tried to hold his breath to listen, but he could not stop his teeth from chattering. After what seemed an eternity he began to once again feel the space around him. The bear was not waking up.

Bears hibernate for approximately 8 months a year and they rarely wake up. They go into a state called a torpor where bodily functions are reduced to about 5% of normal. Bears do not urinate or defecate while in hibernation. When they awake from hibernation, they often are in a stupor for many days, almost appearing to be drunk.

David recalled many years ago when he was hunting moose with his uncle Lloyd. They had come upon a bears den and upon inspection, determined that there was in fact a bear in there. His uncle wanted to shoot the bear so that he could make a bear skin rug. They thought they couldn't shoot the bear sleeping in the den as they would never be able to pull it out. It would be much too heavy. His uncle came up with a plan, that they would return the next day with a rope. They had to wake the bear and get it to come out. His uncle Lloyd would be waiting with his 308 rifle and shoot it. David would crawl down into the hole with a stick to poke the bear and wake it. The rope would be tied around David's ankle and his uncle would pull him out backwards when the bear woke up. It was an insane plan, but they tried it anyway. David was not too keen on crawling down there, but he listened to his uncle. Even with prodding the bear, it would not wake up. They went home empty handed. This gave David hope now that this bear would not wake up.

The cavern was big enough that he could remove his dry sleeping bag from the waterproof bag. The bear slept on. With much difficulty, he pulled his arms out of his parka and removed it. He then opened the zipper on his sleeping bag. With his back to the bear and actually snuggling into the fur, he covered himself with the dry sleeping bag. It felt so good. His body slowly began to warm up and in time he quit shivering and his teeth stopped chattering. The bears body heat was transferring to his own. He had no sense of time, but he finally fell into a deep sleep.

Chapter Six
Reality Check

It was Nov 11th. David woke up in complete darkness. He didn't know how long he had been sleeping. He tried to see the time on his watch, but it was too dark. He was chilled to the bone. His clothes and sleeping bag were not soaking wet but damp. He felt awful. The booze, the cold and the fear made him want to just die right here. He tried to make sense of this all. He knew he was in really bad trouble and odds of surviving were probably slim. The bear hadn't moved a muscle. David could feel the body heat. It had probably saved his life. Without the slow warming, he likely would have died from hypothermia. Think, think, think. What to do next. What do they do in the survival books? Alright, he should take stock. He had good winter boots on. Heavy socks. He had put on long johns- thank god. Undershirt, heavy mackinaw shirt, parka. He didn't know where his gloves were, likely back on the front seat of the truck. There was a hood on his Parka, but he never had his toque on. He had the buck knife on his belt and a pocketknife in his Jeans. He had a lighter in his parka and a second one in his pants. The waterproof matches were still in the truck with the rest of the supplies. He had two granola bars in his Parka pocket. There was his sleeping bag and a waterproof bag to put it in. That was it!

He was very thirsty and hungry as well. He decided to eat one of the granola bars once he got back outside. It would give him some energy and maybe warm him a little. What was the next move? David realized that unless he got in step with the wilderness, the bush would devour him whole. Walking back to the road and town was way too far. He would also have to cross the river again to go back, so that was out of the question. The river had been mostly open where the truck had gone in. There was ice forming on the edges but even in this weather it may take a week or so to freeze over completely. He guessed it might be -7 to -10 Celsius. No, his best bet was to walk to the cabin, rest up, regroup. He was certain there would be some canned and dry foods there like pasta and rice. Once rested and when the river froze over, he could make a game plan to walk out to civilization. He hated to leave the nest in the bears den as it offered a little warmth, but he had to have a bowl movement and he couldn't stay there forever.

He stuffed the waterproof bag full of dry grasses, leaves and twigs that covered the floor in the den. He couldn't tell what was happening outside, but he would have to find a place to get out of the wind and light a fire so that he could warm up and dry out his clothing and sleeping bag. He grabbed his stuff and crawled out of the hole. The daylight was temporarily blinding. The wind was still howling, and the snow was still falling. The first real blizzard of the year. It had snowed at least four or five inches covering all tracks he had made getting here. The day was totally overcast, and he had no compass. He recalled that the road from the bridge went north a couple miles and then made a slow wide arc to the east, almost in the form of a backwards C toward the cabin. He wasn't dead certain of the direction, but if he could cut straight across, he would save valuable time. He would worry about that later. Right now, he had to find some type of a sheltered spot to start a fire. He grabbed a handful of snow and put it in his mouth. He was so thirsty. His watch said 10:30. After getting his parka back on, he zipped up the sleeping bag part way and draped it over his head. Although his clothes were damp, they still had an insulating factor, and the sleeping bag gave him an extra layer of protection from the biting cold. He had no mitts or gloves, so he pulled his hands up his sleeves in the parka to try and keep them warm. He dreaded pulling his pants down to do his business, but there was no choice. He found a log that was about the right height and broke off a couple branches so that he had a space to sit. When he was done, he wiped with his left hand and then tried to clean that by rubbing it in the snow and then on a tree. Gross.

Because it was so overcast and snowing, he more or less guessed at the direction and set off. He was not following any particular trail and the going was slow. Lots of dead fall that he had to go over or around. He continued on for over an hour, his clothes turning to ice, and his teeth were once again chattering. He came to a spot where a plough wind must have gone through. There was a wide swath where trees were all laid over in the same direction. Several of them had pulled up their root system forming a sort of soil wall. He got behind one of these and gathered some branches off the dead trees and started to pile it for a fire. He slowly widened his circle, gathering now some larger pieces of dead wood that would burn substantially longer. Each piece was a struggle. Some ,too long and heavy would have to be abandoned and then search for another one. This all took considerable time and energy. He was totally exhausted from the walk and preparing the wood. His hands were frozen, and he was shaking uncontrollably. He dumped out the dry grasses and leaves from his waterproof sack and then put some of the branches he had gathered on top of them. Before he tried to light the fire, there was one more task. He went out and found 4 poles about two inches in diameter that he could rest up against the root system, and dirt wall that it formed. Over these he would put his wet clothes to dry. He was somewhat out of the wind, but he had no idea if he could keep warm while drying out his clothes.

Thankfully it had stopped snowing. He lit the leaves with his lighter and had no trouble getting a good flame going right away. He put on branches that were a little bigger and soon had an excellent fire going. As the coals got hotter at the base of the fire, he began to remove his clothing. He held his frozen fingers over the flames but not too close, he knew he could burn them easily. His feet felt like two ice blocks. Much to his surprise the back of the wall reflected some heat toward him. He had been smart enough to collect a fairly big pile of wood to burn without going out into the snow for more. David undressed and hung the clothing over the poles above the fire. He pulled the inserts from his boots and hung them up above the fire as well. He wrapped himself in the sleeping bag while his clothes were drying. The heat from the fire felt oh so good. He had to be very close to the fire in order to benefit from its heat He kept turning himself around in a circle, first getting his front side warm and then turn and get his backside warm. In addition, he kept turning his clothes over from one side to the other to distribute the heat evenly. His socks and underwear dried fairly quickly, and he put them back on. Next his long johns, and shirts were dry. It felt wonderful to get them back on and feel the warmth from them. It took a while longer to dry the jeans and the inserts from his boots. His Parka and Boots would take forever, but he forced himself to stay put and let them slowly dry. His instinct was to push on, but he knew enough about the bush to realize you must go slow and think everything through. If panic set in, it could mean the end for him. The fire and the warmth was an achievement for him. It kind of gave him a high. He had dodged the bullet for now.

It was now late afternoon and David decided to make a camp right here. His main objective was to keep that fire going throughout the night so that he wouldn't freeze to death. He dried the damp sleeping bag next. His boots and Parka weren't fully dried, but he put them on and went out to gather more wood. Much more wood! He knew that to keep a fire going all night that he would need a lot. When your cold, alone and in the dark; a fire is like a companion. It sheds light and warmth. Gives you a sense of security and well-being.

He had no axe or saw, so it was a matter of finding dead trees small enough that he could break them up with his hands or by stomping on them with his feet. He also dragged in some small trees with branches on them and tried to make a crude shelter. He leaned them up against the root system which stood about 8 feet high. Darkness was upon him. His next challenge was to find some water, but he couldn't do that tonight. He had never been so thirsty in his life. He found a few small pebbles and put them in his mouth and sucked on them. It created some saliva which was better than nothing. From time to time, he would eat a handful of snow for temporary relief. He wasn't sure if that was good for him, but he did it anyway. He'd read that eating snow will bring down one's body temperature. As the evening wore on, he put down some spruce boughs next to his dirt wall and laid out the sleeping bag on it. He took off his boots and crawled in. It was going to be a long cold night. Every 20 minutes or so he would have to get up and put more wood on the fire. Impossible to get much sleep. His mind drifted to home, Lorenda and his warm bed. He knew no one was going to be worrying about him for a least two weeks. He had told Lorenda and the kids he may even be a little longer than two weeks so not to be concerned because he was well equipped, and he would be careful.

Chapter Seven
No Sleep

Lorenda didn't get much sleep the past two nights. She was really confused about what she was feeling. Was her plan working? What had she done? She wondered if David was safe at the cabin or if he had taken any of the pain killers? He may be dead already. Normal people don't kill their spouses, they go for counselling or they get a divorce, so why did she do what she had done? On the other hand, she was sure that God had spoken to her, telling her that David was planning on getting rid of her. Was that a dream or had that really happened? Perhaps he wouldn't need any painkillers and he would come home safe and sound. If that happened, she would retrieve the Excedrin bottle and dispose of the cyanide pills. Her anxiety was a 10 out of 10 with not knowing what was going on. She felt itchy all over and found herself unconsciously scratching her arms, her face and her hair. When she got home from the Safeway that day, she went straight to the liquor cabinet and poured a gin. She needed to calm her nerves.

Her living room was a comfy space. She loved the hardwood floors and the wide baseboards. The woodwork was dark, warm and inviting. Lorenda flopped down in her big armchair and thought back on her life as she sipped her gin. How had it become so complicated? She remembered back to when she was a child. Her parents had immigrated from Mexico when she was just four years old. They were not well to do by any means, but they provided a safe and happy upbringing. Her father Miguel was a bricklayer and he worked hard and long hours to provide for Lorenda and her two sisters. Grace, her mother had little schooling, but she contributed to the family coffers by cleaning homes. Her older sister Juanita had moved to Chicago when she got married to her husband Michael. He had taken a transfer there and since then, they had not seen each other. They talked on the phone every week or two, but they gradually were drifting apart.

Her younger sister Rosa had gone to university to study law. She had met her future husband there and when they graduated, they were married and moved to Whitehorse. Rosa and Anthony got along well with the Smiths and they visited back and forth a couple times a year. They always got together for Christmas with their parents. Tragically seven years later Rosa was killed in a traffic accident. She and Anthony had been driving home for Christmas from Whitehorse. They had always flown, but this year they decided they wanted to drive. It was a head on collision with a truck. Visibility was poor because it was storming, and they had decided to stop in the next town with a hotel to wait out the weather. They never made it. Anthony was a mess, several broken bones and a collapsed lung. He was in hospital for three weeks, but he recovered. The other driver also died at the scene of the accident.

Lorenda was very close to Rosa and her death was a huge blow. It was about this time that she began to have problems. She began to self- medicate with alcohol and fell into a depression. Eventually she became delusional. She became irritable and often behaved out of character. David tried to be as supportive as possible. Over the next few years there were many trips to see doctors and then psychiatrists. With medication and counselling, Lorenda returned to some form of normality, but it was never quite the same. It had put a huge strain on the marriage. Slowly some of their friends drifted away and they both became withdrawn.

David was no longer the loving husband he once was. It was during this time that Lorenda thought he may be cheating on her. He could come and go from work with no questions asked. He was the boss. She was at work during the day. There was lots of time where she had no idea of what he was doing or where he was.

Lorenda felt bad about the way her life had turned out, but what could she do now? She prayed to god for guidance. He spoke with her. She could hear his voice in her head. God told her not to be hard on herself. It was not her fault. David was planning to do her harm. She was justified in what she had done. She had to take care of herself. Talk to no one about this and leave it up to him. His will would be done. She had nothing to fear. It was much like self defense. No one was to be trusted.

Alright, she felt better now. She poured herself another gin.

Chapter Eight
Lost

It was David's second day in the woods. Nov 12th. More cloud and overcast. No snow but no sun either. David studied the horizon and trees trying to get his bearings. He had no real idea of exactly where he was. He had a hunch he knew the direction he should take. He could only hope he was right.

In about forty minutes of picking his way down a game trail he came upon a ravine with clump birch trees growing in it. He took out his buck knife and cut a strip of bark off one of the Birch trees measuring about a foot square. He fashioned this into a cone structure and put some moss in the bottom. He held it in shape with two of his boot laces wrapped around the perimeter. He then filled it with snow. David had seen this on one of the survival shows that he had watched. He built a small fire and let the cone rest against some stones close to the fire as he warmed himself. In approximately 10 minutes the snow had melted, and he was able to get one good gulp of water. He repeated this process for over an hour until he had quenched his thirst. He felt quite proud of himself that he had come up with this idea. The sky was growing darker. It looked like it may snow again. David pushed on realizing that he would spend another rough night out in the bush.

There were two things that bothered him. He hadn't hit any creeks yet. There were two major creeks in the area that dumped into the Beacon river. Wolf Creek and Bailey Creek. Of course, his map was in the pack sack at the bottom of the river. The second thing, he was in the woods, and he hadn't yet seen a rabbit, a bush grouse, a deer, nothing. However, he realized it had been storming so his chances of seeing animals was diminished. If he didn't get to that cabin soon, he would have to think about hunting, or catching something to eat. His stomach growled. He was getting very hungry and he could feel his body weakening. Everything he did was a struggle. He draped the end of the sleeping bag over his head and trudged on. It was starting to get tattered from catching on branches. He could stay reasonably warm when he was walking, so he decided to roll it up and carry it in the waterproof bag. It was more important to keep the sleeping bag intact.

There was a tree line in the distance that looked taller than the rest. Could that be the riverbank? He headed toward it. He walked on until 3:30. There was a decent spot in thick pines that was fairly sheltered. He had better start setting up camp here. It took quite a while to gather enough firewood for the night. This was really labor intensive because he only had his buck knife to work with. If he had a hatchet or an axe to work with it would be easy. With just the knife he had to break the branches off. Some he hacked at it with the knife. He had no gloves or mitts, so his hands were cut, scratched and full of slivers from the wood. By dark he had a large pile of wood for the fire and about 40 spruce boughs for a bed. His stomach was growling. He still had the one granola bar and he wanted to eat it, but he thought he would eat it in the morning to give him some energy to carry on. Tonight, he got out his birchbark cone and concentrated on re-hydrating.

It was going to be another bone chilling night, but he felt confident that he could stay warm enough to keep from freezing. That meant keeping awake enough to keep the fire stoked. More or less a full-time job. By dark he had built a small wall of branches, mostly to cut the wind. He was heating some fist sized stones in the fire. These he would put between two poles on the ground and then cover the poles with spruce boughs. His bed would be made on top of this and for at least a little while the heat from the rocks would radiate upward warming the spruce boughs and his sleeping bag. He used the waterproof bag for a pillow. It was maybe going down to – 5 or -10 C at night. He had to find that cabin before it got any colder. Tomorrow he would figure out a plan.

He would try to fashion a spear to possibly kill a rabbit or a bush chicken if he saw one. There were spruce grouse and sharp tail grouse that he could attempt to kill if he saw one. He knew he was losing energy and things would only get worse if he didn't get some nourishment in his belly.

The night was cold, but the wind had died right down, and David managed to get some snippets of sleep and keep from freezing in his makeshift bed. Once in the middle of the night he dug out his rocks and re heated them in the fire. He then took a couple of sticks to carry them with and replaced them between the poles under his makeshift bed. This system actually worked fairly well. He dreamt of cozying up to Lorenda's body and feeling the body heat. When he woke in the morning, he didn't want to crawl out of the sleeping bag. He was so grateful that he bought a good sleeping bag. It was rated for -20C and water resistant so the moisture didn't get inside easily.

He melted some snow for water in his birchbark cone and ate the granola bar. It was so good. He couldn't believe how good that could taste and he felt it give him some energy as well. He walked around the perimeter of his little camp until he found a fairly straight young poplar tree about 2 inches in diameter. He hacked it off with his buck knife and fashioned a spear about six feet long. He took his time to sharpen the end and then tried to harden the point in the fire.

It was another grey overcast day, his third day in the bush. Nov 13th. He had noted where the sun had come up and headed in that direction. It should be east. Surely, he would hit one of the old logging roads or a creek that he could follow to hit the Beacon river. He knew the creeks flowed into the Beacon eventually and the Beacon ran downstream into the Hudson's Bay. If he found the river again, he could find the cabin. Then when it froze over completely, he could walk back out to civilization for help. It shouldn't be that difficult, but right now he had no clue of where he was. He started following a game trail through the woods. He carried his sleeping bag in the waterproof bag in front of him with his hands stuck in the middle to keep them warm. He had his spear tucked under his arm and resting on the waterproof bag as well. It was cumbersome and the going seemed slow. As long as he kept walking, he could stay warm. If he stopped for any length of time he would start freezing up. Slow and steady was the answer.

He stopped to rest in a little clearing. Sat down on a fallen log. He ran his fingers through his hair and rubbed his head. He noticed an owl high above in a spruce tree. When he walked on, the owl would fly ahead a little distance and then stop and wait for him to catch up. It was like he was showing David the way. To where he didn't know. The game trail seemed to end into nothing but trees. It was thick in this area.

At 2 P.M. David made his way down an embankment and found a creek flowing at the bottom. Hallelujah! It was flowing at a good rate, so David felt confident that the water was safe to drink. He knelt on a log a put his face in the water. It was ice cold, but he drank until his stomach could hold no more. David felt that things were improving. It lifted his spirits. Perhaps he could follow the flow of the water and find the Beacon. He moved on, picking his way through the willows. In a short time, he came to where a large pine had fallen over. The root system formed a wall of dirt and moss as it was ripped up from the ground. This wall was over six feet high and the ground at its base was flat. It would make an excellent camp site and fresh water nearby to boot. David made a fire in the flat spot and for the remainder of the day gathered firewood and dragged in poles to improve his shelter. He spent some time finding some rocks so that he could heat them for his bed. It was dark and he was exhausted. He climbed back into the sleeping bag and dozed off listening to the timber wolves howling in the night. He was definitely getting his survival test!

Chapter Nine
Nourishment

After a cold and almost sleepless night, David got up, restoked the fire and warmed himself. He had survived another night. His thirst dictated that he go to the stream and drink his fill. He came back to the fire to think about how to proceed. He was so hungry and getting weaker. Everything was such an effort. Just then he heard something in the willows. He slowly got up and picked up his spear. Very slowly and as quietly as possible he went toward the sound. There was a sharp tail grouse picking in the leaves, under a tall pine tree. He advanced ever so slowly. When he got a little closer, the grouse would flutter off a couple yards. He advanced again, grouse flies off a few feet and then walks slowly getting into cover. This "dance" was repeated for almost a half hour and finally David was in a position to try and spear the bird. He threw the spear as hard as he could, and it struck the grouse in the side. It didn't kill the bird, but it stunned him enough that it gave David enough time to run up and grab the grouse as it was kicking around in the leaves like a chicken with his head cut off. David rung the grouse's neck and it went limp. He almost did his own dance he was so happy. Food! There is not a lot of meat on a grouse, but it was a meal. The first one that he would have in four days! He was elated.

He made his way back to his little camp and re stoked the fire. He took the bird down to the stream and dressed it with his jackknife and then searched around until he found a flat stone that he could cook the bird on. He washed the flat rock well in the stream and then built a sort of rectangular fireplace of stones with the flat rock on top and where he could shove sticks underneath and then cook the bird. The next hour was heaven. He ate every morsel and sucked every little bone clean. It was too late to move on, so he would gather more firewood and spend another night here with food in his belly! It was like he was on steroids. The highs were very high, and the lows were very low.

David awoke to a light snow fall. It was his 5th day lost in the woods. He thought it was Nov 15th, but he was beginning to lose track of time. A small plane passed overhead. It was not close enough to get him excited, but there was a slight chance the pilot might see the smoke from David's fire and come over to investigate. He built up the fire and went out to gather more firewood. There was lots of dead trees fallen, but it was time consuming as he had no axe. He had to do it, if he was to stay warm. Since he had no idea where he was or where he was going, he decided to stay put for a day. David was feeling a little more optimistic. He made more plans.

He would build a signal fire to be lit if another small aircraft might pass by. David had lost sense of time, but he knew no one would be looking for him as it had been less than a week since he had left home. He would also look for a clearing in order to fashion a large SOS that might be seen from above. In addition, he had got a Sharp tail grouse, so there was bound to be more in the area. He spent the morning improving his camp site. A few more trees and branches to cover in his shelter. He gathered more stones and built a wall behind the fire to reflect heat into his sleeping area. He spent an hour cutting and bringing in more spruce boughs to soften the makeshift bed and to provide more warmth.

In the afternoon he took his spear and set out to see if he could find a grass slough or some sort of clearing to build a S.O.S out of small trees or branches. He walked for a couple of hours but found nothing. He always kept the stream in sight or nearby so that he wouldn't get lost. Once he saw another sharp tail but failed to hit it with his spear. It finally flew far enough away that he could no longer find it. It was a blow, but perhaps he would see another. He needed food badly. Three times during the afternoon, he made his way down to the creek and although it was now covered with a thin layer of ice, there were always spots where the water bubbled through. He could easily break the ice surface with a pole as well in order to drink. He was at least staying hydrated. Every small achievement kept him positive and moving on. By the time he got back to his camp site, the fire was out and had to be restarted. He was totally exhausted. Nothing left to do but to crawl into his sleeping bag and try to get some rest. He fell into a deep, deep sleep.

The morning sun rise woke him. He ran his fingers through his hair and rubbed his head. David decided to try to keep some track of time. He cut off a small piece of a willow tree and carved six notches in it. It should be Nov 16th. His fire was out, and he was cold. He rubbed his body with his hands to warm himself and get the blood flowing. His feet were like ice. Once again there were critical decisions to make.

The sun rose there, that was east. He wanted to head in an easterly direction, but the flow of the creek was angled north or north east he thought. His stomach was hurting. He was so hungry. Moving through this bush in cold weather ate up a lot of calories and energy. He decided to stay put for another day, try to find and kill another grouse, rest, and make his sleeping shelter a little warmer. He went out and gathered more firewood for the night. All the while his mind was working on his problem. He should be within a day's walk of that cabin he thought. Tomorrow he would head toward the sun and leave the creek if need be. If he didn't find that cabin soon, he knew his chances of survival were getting slimmer. After restarting his fire and warming himself, he set off with his spear in hand. He was really worried that if he got lost and could not find his way back to the sleeping bag and camp, that would surely be the end of him. He studied the ground constantly and he marked some trees with his buck knife as he went.

There were lots of deer tracks, tracks left by mice and squirrels, rabbit tracks. He saw a mouse scurrying across the snow from one tunnel to another. Too fast to hit it with his spear. Several times he saw squirrels in the trees, but he had no means of setting a snare, no wire to work with. He was not sure if he had the know how to set a proper snare anyway. The squirrels never stayed still long enough to throw the spear and lots of the time they were too high up in the trees. If he kept moving slowly, he was able to stay reasonably warm.

Up ahead he saw something dark in the snow. There were tracks all over. Looked like maybe wolf tracks. Several birds were circling and landing. It must be some kind of a kill he reasoned. He approached the dark spot cautiously. Now he could see that it was a deer or perhaps a small moose laying there. Hair and blood splatter covered the snow all around the carcass. As he got closer, he saw it was a young moose. It was nearly all eaten but there was flesh yet around the hind legs, the neck, and one front leg. He stood and scanned the trees around him. Were the wolves still nearby? David was frozen with fear. If they saw him would they attack? All he had was his buck knife, and a home-made spear to defend himself. He had never heard of a wolf attacking a man. Still, he was shaking in his boots. He knew if the wolves were in a pack and they were hungry enough, they may attack. He slowly and quietly knelt by the carcass. With his knife he began to cut away strips of flesh off the bones. The meat seemed very stiff but not frozen solid. The kill must have been last night. He stuffed the meat into his parka pockets until he could not get any more in. He put a small piece in his mouth. Once again, he scanned the perimeter of the trees around. He saw nor heard anything.

As quickly as he could without running, he began to retrace his footsteps in the snow toward his camp. He knew those wolves would not be far away from their kill. His heart was pounding in his chest from the fear of the wolves and from the anticipation of eating the moose meat. With new energy from his adrenaline pumping, he made his way back to his camp.

With his campfire crackling, he sharpened a few willow sticks and hung a couple of the meat pieces over the fire to roast. He slipped down to the creek and broke a hole in the ice, drank deeply and filled his bark cone/ cup with water. He was salivating and could hardly wait for the meat to cook. The first piece he tried was burnt on the outside and still raw in the middle, but it tasted heavenly. It was food. David nearly cried. He took a flat rock from the little rock wall he had built at the back of his fire. Again, he fashioned a small stove in order that he could cook the meat on top the rock, turning it over every 5 minutes or so. In this fashion the meat cooked more thoroughly and didn't burn on the outside. As he cooked, he kept eating the strips of meat that he had cooked on the willow sticks. He ate until he was full. His stomach had shrunk a fair bit, so he couldn't eat all that much. He almost felt sick to his stomach but fought to keep it down so that he would benefit from the nourishment. The full stomach made him sleepy, and he had a pretty good stock of firewood, so he built up the fire and crawled into his sleeping bag. He felt full and soon was sleeping. He dreamed he was in bed with Lorenda. He had the small of his back against her ass and her body heat was warming him. He never wanted to wake. He just wanted to soak up this wonderful feeling. Peaceful and safe.

He felt sorry that he was not more understanding and loving toward Lorenda. When she started to have problems, he was not very sympathetic. He was cold toward her and felt she should be strong enough to work through her problems. He had distanced himself from her. Was that what a husband was supposed to do?

In reflection, he knew he was wrong. He missed her now.

When he woke up it was dark. He could hear the wolves howling in the distance. The fire was nearly out but there were still some hot embers. He carefully put some more sticks on the fire and re kindled it. He did not want to use his two lighters unless he had to. He put more moose meat on the rock to cook. He thought about the bear that had warmed his body. That almost seemed unreal, like a dream. Stumbling into the bears den had no doubt saved his life. He thought about the wolves. In a way they had fed him. The sharp tail grouse had presented itself so that he could eat. He began to think that he was getting help from nature. He felt more confident he could get out of this mess. He had little to work with, he had no gloves and when the weather turned colder, he would be in real trouble.

He had to find that cabin if he was to survive. He ate again and it didn't take much to fill him. The meat was so tasty. He relished every single bite. He emptied his pockets and set out piles of meat approximately one meal in size. He had four piles. He decided that he would have one meal each morning unless he was able to get more food. He built up the fire and crawled back into the sleeping bag.

Chapter Ten
Lorenda's Head

Lorenda had a feeling of impending doom. She imagined herself sitting in a prison cell. Convicted of murdering her husband. They had found David's body and an autopsy revealed it was cyanide poisoning. They pinned it on her because Cindy had told them about her visit and the police were able to put two and two together. Cindy was not to be trusted. No one was to be trusted. They were all working against her, but why? What had she done? She didn't deserve this.

That day at work ,Lorenda noticed that people were always looking at her. Watching her every move. Did they know something? Her boss noticed that she seemed agitated and asked if she needed the day off. Lorenda accepted, grateful to avoid everyone watching her.

When she arrived home and looked around, she couldn't believe the state of the house. Normally she kept everything very orderly and clean. As she looked around, she saw dirty dishes in the sink. Obviously, no one had swept or vacuumed this week. There were discarded clothes lying here and there. Magazines on the floor by the couch. Why hadn't she noticed this before? That was odd. It seemed like someone else had been living here, not her. She had to get a grip on things. She poured herself a gin and tonic, then started cleaning. This would never do.

She cleaned the house for the next four hours. The music was turned up loud and she got herself into a better head space. When she was done, she called her mom and talked for almost an hour. She then called Juanita and did the same. She tried to keep the conversations as normal as possible so they wouldn't worry about her. She felt much better.

For the first time in days, she cooked herself a decent meal. Ham, scalloped potatoes, peas and a lettuce salad. Lorenda opened a bottle of red wine to have with her supper. It was a wine from Portugal, expensive. She treated herself.

CHAPTER ELEVEN
The Shack

In the morning, the wind had picked up again and once again it was snowing. It definitely felt colder as well. The temperature was dropping. David built up the fire and cooked another ration on his makeshift stone stove. Seventh day in the bush. It must be Nov17th. According to his little whittled stick calendar. He wrestled with his next move as he ate. The plain moose meat with no seasonings still tasted like prime rib to him. It was food. He didn't know if he wanted to leave this site just yet. When it was snowing, he found it hard to determine which way he was going. He was lost anyway, but he thought maybe he would be more lost if he carried on, if that was possible. More lost?

The landscape here was not quite as thick with trees. It was a mixture of spruce, poplar, and birch. The terrain was flat. He decided that this morning he would try to improve his camp a little. Get more pine boughs for his bed. Work on improving the wind break around the fire and his sleeping area. Stones were hard to find, but he could use branches and small logs. He could also scoop some snow into the waterproof bag and then bank his shelter with the snow to insulate the shelter and keep out the wind. He was pretty much out of firewood, so that would take two or three hours to replenish. If time allowed in the afternoon, he would try to make it back to the moose kill and hopefully get more meat. While he walked to gather firewood, he found it harder to keep his hands warm. The temperature now must be more than 10 degrees below freezing. He had numerous cuts, scratches, and slivers on his hands. He was limited to breaking up dead fallen trees for his firewood. He thought the river would fully be frozen over by now, that's if he ever found the river again.

At noon, he built the fire larger, but the wind made it more difficult to warm himself. He decided to go for the moose kill. He could keep warm by walking and maybe by the time he returned to his camp, the wind would go down. The snow was filling in the tracks and two or three times he had to search for the tracks he had made the day before. By 2 p.m. he found the kill once again, but the bones had been picked clean by the birds. Not an ounce of meat left. Disheartened, he turned around and headed back toward his little camp. The wind was not subsiding, and the snow was steadily falling. He spotted a grouse in some willows, but he was not carrying his spear. He got close enough to throw his knife at it, but he missed, and the bird flew off and hid in the thickets. It took him a few minutes to find the knife and he didn't see the grouse again, so he abandoned the hunt, as he was anxious to get back to his fire and sleeping bag before dark. If he got lost in the dark, it could and likely would spell disaster. His survival depended on him being super careful and making the right decisions.

He followed his tracks back to the camp. He got there in time. 20 or 30 minutes more would have made it very difficult to see. There were still some hot embers in the fireplace, and he rekindled the fire once more. He was glad he had worked on his bed and wind break. It seemed to help a little. He wrestled with the idea of eating the last of the moose meat. He knew he shouldn't as he had no idea of when and where the next meal would come from. Fuck it. He couldn't get the moose meat out of his mind, so he sat by the fire and cooked the remaining portion. He ate it very slowly, savouring every bite. At least he would go to bed with his hunger at least somewhat satisfied. He crawled into the sleeping bag and fell into a deep sleep.

He had a dream that he had had several times before. In the dream, he was a young boy, perhaps seven or eight years old. It was maybe the seventeen or eighteen hundreds. The place was in England, he didn't know where, but maybe London. He was running away from two men. The streets were cobblestone. There were gas lantern poles. The buildings all looked like two or three storey structures and appeared to be built of stone. The people on the streets were dressed poorly. Horses pulled carts along. The men were chasing him because he had stolen something, and they were gaining on him. He ducked into a livery stable and ran to the back of the building and quickly covered himself with hay. The men bolted in searching the stalls as they made their way to the back and then they found him. He was terribly frightened. This is where he always woke up. Maybe because he didn't want to find out what happened next. The dream was always exactly the same. David wondered if he was recalling a past life. He had read somewhere that dreams were to teach you something. How was this dream relevant to his life or the situation he was in now?

When he woke, he wondered how the boys were doing? Neither one of them was setting the world on fire. They both drank too much. It was frustrating to watch them ruining their lives. He wondered if the way they lived was because of the way they were brought up. Not really. He had always tried to be a good father. David felt as if he and Lorenda had failed somehow. He knew it was partially the times they lived in. When he was growing up, kids were taught how to earn money and contribute to the family's welfare. They were taught how to save if they wanted to purchase something. These days people wanted everything right now. They didn't worry about savings. If there was room on the credit card, they spent. Mortgaged their homes to the max. No planning for retirement. He wondered what was going to happen to them. He wished he had been successful in teaching them money management, but they chose not to listen.

Well, he wasn't going to waste any more time worrying about them. He had wanted an adventure and to test his survival skills when he had planned this trip. He had gotten his wish. His survival skills were definitely being tested. He had to concentrate on the present if he was to have a chance to survive.

He noticed an owl perched in a tree. Was this the same owl? Would it lead him in the right direction? He wondered if he was losing his mind. Owls don't normally lead humans to safety, but maybe he should follow it anyway. He wasn't doing so well on his own. He had this creek and logic said he should follow it, but maybe he should gamble and follow the direction the owl flew to. After all, hadn't the bear saved him, and the wolves fed him? He was really torn on what to do. He wanted to stay at this little encampment and stay warm, but he had to get going. The owl moved off and he noted the direction in which it flew. He felt lightheaded and he didn't know what the hell was going on, but he gathered his sleeping bag, the spear and the waterproof bag and headed off in the direction dictated by the owl. Every 10 or 15 minutes he would catch site of the owl again. It seemed to be watching him and waiting for him to catch up.

Around noon he broke thru on to what seemed to be a man-made trail. It looked wider than a game trail. He soon saw a tree that had been cut with a chain saw. One saw cut on the left of the trail and one on the right. In the bush were a couple of sections of the log. His heart was racing! This is the first real sign of man that he had come upon. The log had been cut many years ago, but it definitely was either a ski doo trail or a walking path used by a trapper or maybe hunters that had been in the district. He now had to decide right or left? He looked for his owl, but it was nowhere to be seen. David was not a religious person, but now he prayed to God for guidance. He realized that in an hour or two he would once again have to look for a good spot to shelter. He was freezing cold and so he built a small fire to warm his hands. His stomach was growling. He was really thirsty. He was excited about the trail, but he was again feeling the effects of little food. He was just about to head off to his right when he spotted the owl to his left , up the trail a bit. Then left it would be he decided. He silently thanked God. He felt as though this was divine intervention. He was being helped.

David was raised a catholic, and his parents always took him and his siblings to church on Sundays. He received the sacraments and went to Sunday school. Catechism they called it. The boys wore black pants and white shirts when they attended. The girls had a uniform and were all dressed the same.

The nuns who taught them, put the fear of the lord in them. If they didn't obey the commandments, they would surely burn in hell for eternity. The steaks were high for sure.

In his adult life, David and Lorenda went to church less often. As the allegations of sexual abuse by the priests came out, they quit going all together.

Now when his life was on the line, David found himself returning to his God. He needed him. He felt this experience was renewing him. It was changing him. It was challenging him to think about the choices he had made in his life. If he survived, he was going to change. Be more grateful for what he had. He would spend more time with his boys and their families and certainly be more understanding and loving toward his wife.

The walking was much easier on the trail. No longer were there branches catching the sleeping bag. Far fewer logs to step over or go around. In around 45 minutes he came to another creek. A much larger one with a beaver dam built across. He had lost site of the owl. He hadn't had a drink of water since early morning and at the top of the beaver dam, where it crossed the creek; water ran freely in a little channel about a foot wide. It looked like an Otter run. David could see where the otter slid over the top and the mud was packed down on the slide. He walked carefully on the top of the dam to the open water. He knew from experience if he fell into the creek on the downside, the deep side, the water could be 8 or 10 ft. deep. He knelt down and drank deeply for several minutes until he could drink no more. He crossed the creek on the dam and continued down the trail.

He noticed several tracks of deer, rabbits, bush chickens and what he thought might be a lynx track. It was getting dark, and he was getting pretty chilled. He started looking for a place to sleep for the night. No time now to build much of a shelter. The pines were bigger here, and he may just sleep under a large pine tree. If it snowed, at least he would stay dry. Then as he crunched through the snow, which was about a foot deep here, he saw something in the distance that looked like a building. He hurried on; his heart was pounding. He tripped on a small tree crossing the path and fell heavily. He picked himself up running ahead and left his spear and the sleeping bag behind. He ran toward the building. Just off to the left-hand side of the path stood an old shack. It was made of logs, obviously very old by the look of it. It was probably 6 ft wide and 10 ft. long. Maybe 6 ft high in the centre. It had a wooden door and a window. The glass in the window was very dirty, but still intact. There used to be tar paper on the roof, but 95 percent of it had rotted off and blown away. Rough-hewn planks were still there, one corner had fallen in. An old rusty chimney crowned the old trappers shack. David was so excited, he almost pissed himself. The door was shut, held closed by a stick of wood with a large nail through it. He opened the door and peered inside. The rusty old hinges creaked. It was dark inside but with the door opened he could see an old airtight stove, a framework that acted as a bed, an old home-made table, and one chair that looked like it was bought in a store, not homemade. It had spirals on the uprights. Two wood planks still on the wall above the window acted as shelves. Some old cans on the shelves. Just below the window was the table, obviously placed there so the light from the window would shine on it. A broken coal oil lantern was on the floor under the table. There was piles of shredded cloth on the floor. No doubt an old sleeping bag shredded by squirrels or mice. The little cabin had a very dank smell. No one had opened that door for years.

David sat on the dusty chair and rested for a few minutes. His mind was going 90 miles an hour. Okay first things first. He would go back and retrieve his sleeping bag. Then go get some wood and see if he could get that stove lit. The stove pipes had fallen down but it looked like they all may be there. He went outside, it was getting dark. He found a little path going down an embankment and not too far was another little stream. Water! No doubt the overnight cabin was built here for that reason. He collected an armful of small branches and took them up to the cabin. He then reassembled the stove pipes. It was a bit of a jigsaw puzzle, but he finally got them together. They were rusty and there were holes in them, but that's all he had. It was now dark. He broke up some kindling and lit the fire. He thought, thank god the lighters still had fluid. Without fire he was done. The bottom of the little airtight stove was almost rusted out and hot ashes were spilling out on to the floor. That wouldn't do. There would be a fire started on the floor in no time. David looked around the cabin for something to put under the stove. He couldn't find anything. He went outside and looked around the cabin. Against the back wall was a pan, maybe 18 inches by 24 inches. It was rusty, but it would work. He slid it under the airtight. Smoke slowly filled the cabin, but as the stove got hotter the smoke carried up the pipes better. He had to keep the door open for the first 20 minutes but slowly the air cleared.

The cabin was dark, but a little bit of light crept through from the stove. He spread the sleeping bag over the bare planks of the bed. He had nothing to eat, but he took his birch cone and went out and picked his way through the dark to the little stream. He again drank his fill and brought a full container back to the little cabin. He would examine those tin cans in the morning. He doubted there could be anything in them and they looked pretty rusty. Exhausted, he took off his boots and crawled into the sleeping bag. He was off the ground, dry, no wind, and heat coming from the small airtight stove. He was in heaven! He rolled up the waterproof bag to use as a pillow and lay his head down. For now, he was rescued. His prayers were answered. As he was falling asleep, he wondered if this was all a dream. It almost didn't seem real.

Chapter Twelve
The Cabin.

This was his ninth day in the bush. According to his stick calendar, it should be Nov 18th. When he crawled out of the sleeping bag, the fire was out, and the cabin was cold. His joints ached. He went outside to pee. He noted that his pants were fitting pretty loosely around his waist. He was definitely losing weight. Man was he hungry. He was getting a good beard and mustache going. His joints ached and he felt sick, but at the same time was pretty excited. With a little work he could soften that bed with a grass mattress and or some spruce boughs. He would cover the hole in the roof where it had fallen in, to keep more of the heat in. He would spend today gathering firewood for the stove and doing his best to get some food someway. He had seen several rabbit tracks, also some of bush chickens and there were always squirrels everywhere. He just didn't know how to get them.

This was an overnight cabin, built years ago before there were all terrain vehicles or snow machines. It would have been used by a trapper working his line. Often, they would build a shelter like this a day's walk from the main camp so that they could check and set traps for a day, stay overnight and then return to the main camp by the same route or an alternate route. Often times the route formed more or less a circle with the overnight camp in the middle. It also could have been erected as a hunting shack. Whatever the case, David felt pretty certain that in one direction or the other he would find the main trapper's cabin. He decided to spend one more day here to rest up, hopefully find a meal and then strike out.

He re lit the stove and then went out to gather wood. The third time out for wood he spotted a sharp tail grouse. He did not have his spear along, but he always had the buck knife on his belt. He very slowly tried to close the distance between himself and the bird. Each time he was ready to throw the knife, the grouse would move a little further away. This game went on for over twenty minutes. Finally, he had an open try. He hurled the knife but missed by about 4 inches. The grouse flew off. Bush chickens cannot fly any long distance, so it did not go far. The hunt resumed consuming another 15 minutes. David made a second attempt without being successful. Then a third. Missed again. He figured the grouse would stay in the area, so he gave up and carried another arm full of wood to the cabin. He wanted to have at least twice as much as he needed for the night. He wanted to be toasty warm for a change. He broke off some spruce boughs and put them on the bed frame. He then found a couple poles to bridge the hole in the roof and put spruce branches across them to close over the hole in the roof. He went to the little stream and drank his fill and then filled his waterproof bag with grasses and brought them to the cabin to make himself a little nest on the bed. He was exhausted. He kept feeding the fire in the airtight stove to keep the cabin toasty warm. The beauty of the airtight was that it had an air vent that you could open or close to regulate the burn of the fire. Less air going in made the wood burn slower and his wood pile would go a lot further than an open fire.

It was now mid-afternoon. Cold but sunny. He rested a bit. Should he go try to find that sharp tail or comb through the garbage pile that was just over the bank. He may be able to find something useful before dark. He would love to have a container to boil water in. Just about every cabin in the woods had a garbage heap within a minute of the cabin where the used tins, bottles, plastic bags, etc. were thrown. This cabin was no exception. He noticed the pile when he had walked down to the little brook.

David spent the next hour sifting through the garbage. There were lots of whiskey and beer bottles. Tons of rusty tin cans, old pots, rusted frying pans, bed springs, two or three burnt out lamps. The only thing he found that would be useful was two bottles that had screw on caps. They were 40 oz whiskey bottles. Canadian club and 5 Star. Now he could carry water with him. He went to the stream and rinsed the bottles several times and then filled them both and retreated to the heat of the cabin. It was growing dark and so he stayed inside. Fourteen hours till daylight again. Lots of time to think. Nothing to eat, but at least he had water. If he lifted the lid a bit on the airtight, it provided a little light. It was just nicer than sitting in the dark.

The nights in the forest, although David knew there was basically nothing here to fear, were still unsettling. There is something about the dark that unnerves you. The sounds of trees creaking and cracking from the cold. The wind.

From the little light emitted by the stove, he saw a mouse on the window ledge. He grabbed his spear and swatted at it. Bingo, hit it and it was dead. His first instinct was to cook the small amount of meat and eat it, but he calmed his mind and thought that this mouse could be bait for something bigger. He had to eat soon. If he had some wire, he could try to make some snares for squirrels, but no wire. No traps, no nothing, but he had a mouse. Wolves ate mice, foxes ate mice, so did weasels, marten and fishers. While going through the trash he had seen a half-buried wooden box. It looked like it might have been used on the back of a quad or ski doo to carry gear. He could make a drop trap from this. If he placed the mouse inside the box and somehow tied a thread to it and then attached that to a stick that balanced the box held upright and upside down, he may just be successful in catching something he could kill and eat. The success would come from a perfect balance of that box on the stick. In the morning he would dig out the box and see if it was plausible.

He was excited! Maybe something to eat. Another mouse on the windowsill. Another kill. This repeated six times until he went to sleep in a warm cabin at about 9:30 P.M.

Chapter Thirteen
The Trapper

It was his tenth day in the bush. The morning brought warmer temperatures. He stepped out of the little cabin and looked at the sun. It was a clear day. Noticeably warmer. Great day for walking. He tried to determine the directions from where the sun rose. It looked like the trail here ran east and west. He kind of hoped that it would be north and south. He didn't know for sure, but he thought he may be North of Pete's cabin. He hoped that trail was one that would take him south to the cabin he was looking for. It should be within a day's walk, like maybe five or six hours. Years ago, when trappers walked their lines, they often built little out camps. Shelters that they could stay overnight in, to keep warm, cook a meal, get some sleep and then carry on. At the very most the main camp might be two days walk, as the trapper may have two out camps. He was sure it was not more than that. He had spent time up in this country before. He had come upon one of these out camps, or overnight cabins while hunting. He knew he had to be close. Still, he still could not figure out why he had not hit the river. That was a puzzle. His mind worked constantly on that and he could not shut it off. He wanted to set off. He knew if he found the cabin, it would have some canned goods like beans and canned vegetables. It would have macaroni, noodles, maybe chicken noodle soup, perhaps even canned coffee, sugar, salt, flour, and who knows what. He couldn't wait to find it. He thought he must be fairly close. It started to snow again. He really had to restrain his instinct to go but he decided to try to use the six mice to catch something.

He went and dug out the wood box from the garbage. It looked like maybe an old coke box. Fairly heavy wood and two handles carved out from the sides. He found a spot under a big pine tree about 100 yards from the cabin and set up the trap. He had cut two mice in half, with guts exposed. That should carry a scent. Now he had to decide, go right and back across that creek or go left and find out where the trail led from here. It was impossible to know which way was the right way. If his theory was correct either way would lead back to the main cabin. He believed the trail would form a loop. He would check the trap later in the day, and tomorrow he would set off, no matter what the weather. He was desperate to get something into his stomach. He refilled the water bottles and then skinned and fleshed two mice with his pocketknife. He roasted the small amount of meat on top the rusty airtight stove and slowly ate the little bits of meat. Oh, it was so good, but such a small amount. He couldn't help himself. He did the same with the two remaining mice. Little as it was, it was somewhat satisfying. His stomach had shrunk so small, it didn't take much to fill it. Not that it was anywhere close to being filled.

Next it was out again to replenish the wood pile. He gathered small wood. Dry, dead wood that was one or two inches in diameter. Easily broken off with your bare hands as he had no axe or hatchet. He lay down for about 40 minutes and then went out to check his box trap. Before he got there, he saw that it had moved! There was something inside the box! It had fallen! The trap had worked. There was something making noises, like a hissing from inside the box. David quickly ran up and stood on top the box to make sure that whatever was in there was not going to get out. He took out the buck knife from his sheaf. Whatever was in there was going to be a meal, if he didn't let it get away. He lifted the corner of the box slightly, the animal inside poked his nose through the slit of an opening, scratching away; trying desperately to get out. He opened it just a bit more until the whole head came out. Then he jumped back on top the box. His weight cut off the animal's air. He had his weight on the throat. It was not long before the kicking and scratching stopped. He waited an extra minute until the animal was completely still. No sound or movement. Then he lifted the box. It was a fisher. What a beautiful site. Supper!

A fisher is a small carnivorous mammal who lives in the boreal forest. An adult weighs about seven pounds. Their fur is darker than a Marten. A dark brown. It normally eats small rodents and squirrels. It also eats birds, eggs and even porcupines.

Oh my god. His stomach was going to be completely full. He took the animal and the box back to the little cabin. He skinned the fisher, then gutted it. He took it down to the stream and washed it thoroughly. His hands were freezing. He stoked the fire in the airtight, nice and hot. He wished he had a pot, a frying pan, some tin foil, anything to cook on. Since he had nothing, he would just have to put the carcass on the rusty top of the stove and cook it that way. He stayed close to the stove, keeping it stoked and turning the body of the fisher over often to try to cook it evenly. When he thought it was cooked, he took his knife to wipe away the rust and began to peel away strips of meat. It had a weird taste, but it was food, and it filled his stomach. He ate greedily until his stomach was full, overfull. He then stoked the fire and crawled into his sleeping bag. It was nice and warm in the little cabin. Dark.

His mind felt like he was really drunk or on drugs. He passed out into a very deep sleep. Throughout the night, he awoke many times. He was sexually aroused for some reason. He had dreams of his wife, of women that he had known and wished he had gone to bed with. Not to make love, but to have sex. He filled the airtight stove, he slept, he dreamed of naked women. Women that he had never seen naked, but wished he had. It was a very long and weird night. Perhaps something in the fisher meat?

CHAPTER FOURTEEN
Down the trail

The morning of Nov 20th, he ate more fisher meat for breakfast. He had been lost now for 11 days. He wished for, and visualized peas, corn, potatoes, fruit and deserts. Chocolate cake, brownies, pumpkin pie heaped with ice cream. The fisher meat was not half bad tasting, and it filled his belly. He cut the remainder of the meat into bite size chunks and stuffed them into his coat pockets. It would have been nice to have a plastic bag to put the meat into, but of course he had nothing. He took his water bottles and went to the stream to fill them. Next, he wrapped them in the sleeping bag and then stuffed it all into the waterproof bag. Before David left, he gathered and broke up some more kindling. He placed it by the stove, just in case he had to return for some reason. He grabbed his spear and set out. He was most anxious to find the main cabin and he couldn't be too far away. It was always a chore to keep his hands warm as he had no mitts. A good pair of gloves would make his journey so much easier. He had to stop and stuff his hands into his arm pits or build a small fire and warm them, to keep them from freezing.

He was totally concentrating on survival. He had lost a lot of weight and didn't have much energy or stamina, but the fisher meat had helped a lot. So, had the little cabin and warm sleeps. That had helped a lot and it built his confidence that he could and would survive out here. It was just a matter of finding Pete's cabin. Once he found it, he would regain his strength and then be able to follow the trails out to civilization and get back home.

The snow was crunchy under his boots. Except for birds, the bush was silent as he walked. There were tracks here, there, and everywhere as he made his way. He was constantly looking out over the bush for something that he might recognize. At noon he stopped by a small creek and made a fire to warm himself. He ate a couple more pieces of the meat and drank some water. A woodpecker tapped away on a dead tree. What creek was this? Where did it go? He spotted a sharp tail grouse on the other side of the creek but didn't have the energy to go after it. He was anxious to push on and find that cabin. It would be his salvation. He set off again, pacing himself so that he would not tire out. He saw a pair of whiskey jacks. He took that as a good sign as they often hung around trapper's cabins.

    At about 2 pm he came to a T in the path. The trail he was walking on intersected with another. Again, he could go right or left. He sat down to rest and warm his hands. He heard a plane going over, but it was not close enough to try to signal in any way. David was starting to feel some anxiety. He had to find that cabin before dark or he was fucked. Maybe 3 hours of daylight left. He ran his fingers through his hair and rubbed his head.

    No man tracks, no ski doo tracks. He hadn't really expected to see any, but one could always hope. It was cold but not brutal. Perhaps- 5 or -10 Celsius. He was on the verge of panic. Shit, Shit, Shit. He needed a break. Please God let me find that cabin he thought. He began to pray. Lord help me to make the right decision here. Left, or right? He decided on right.

    He was so tired, not a lot of energy to draw on. He trudged on. Every step a bit of a struggle. It was getting dark now. He had crossed 2 more small streams. They were so small he could just jump across them. The trail was getting harder to follow. It seemed to have narrowed and was more grown in. He ate a couple more pieces of meat to try to put some gas in his tank. It was 4:30 now. It would be dark in a half hour. This was not the trail to the cabin. It was too small, too narrow. Where the fuck was that river? He had no idea what direction he was walking in. Panic was setting in. He had no shelter built for the night. He dreaded the idea of sleeping out in the rough, in the cold. Would he freeze to death? Tears began to roll down his cheeks. He sobbed. He stopped and curled into a ball on the ground in the snow. Fuck, fuck, fuck, and fuck. He was going to die here. After 10 or 15 minutes, the sobbing stopped. He ate more meat. As long as he kept moving, perhaps he would not freeze. He decided to turn around and try to retrace his steps. It would be very difficult in the dark. Maybe if he was super careful, he could do it. He drank some more water and set off once more, this time in the dark.

Chapter Fifteen
Return to safety

David fought to control his anxiety. He accessed his situation. He had been walking since about 10 A.M. and now it was 5:45. Almost 8 hours. He was tired and didn't think he would keep up the same pace, plus it was dark so picking his way down the trail would definitely be slower. If he didn't get lost that would put him back at the out camp by maybe 3 or 4 in the morning. He ate the last 3 pieces of his meat. He only had three quarters of a bottle of water left, but he had crossed a couple streams, so they could be refilled. There was a three-quarter moon and not too many clouds so seeing the trail and his footprints was possible, but not easy. The night felt spooky and, in the distance, he could hear an owl. Was it the same owl calling him? He thought if he did lose the trail, he would go toward the owl's call. He trusted it. One foot in front of the other. A sense of calm came over him as he plugged along. He kept hearing things in the bush. Animals moving about no doubt. He was not afraid, as he was sure that nothing would attack him. The only exceptions possibly, would be an animal with rabies or a pack of timber wolves that were very hungry. Chances of that were slim, but it always preyed on his mind. He had seen no wolf tracks all day. He retraced his steps to the small stream. Here he took a break. He refilled the water bottles and drank his fill. He was not certain that the water was safe to drink, however he had no choice and so far, it had given him no problems. His legs were cold and his hands nearly frozen, so he gathered some dead branches and made a small fire to warm himself. The lighters were still working, but at some time the fuel would run out. That would be a death sentence.

After a 20- minute rest, and getting some feeling back in his hands, he moved on. He wished he could just stop and lay down. He was exhausted. Eventually he found his way back to the T in the trail. He stopped to drink but his water bottles were gone. He had either left them by the last fire he had made, or they had somehow dropped out of the sleeping bag. That was bad but not the end of the world. Keep moving. He estimated he had another 4 to 5 hours back to the little cabin. It seemed insurmountable, but he dug deep and moved on. At least he was still on the trail. The trek became a hazy dream. David began to stumble. He wasn't lifting his feet enough and every tree or branch across the trail tripped him up. On one fall, he hit his head on a log and the blood trickled down his forehead onto his cheek. He remembered little after that. Just put one foot in front of the other, he kept thinking. At 4:30 A.M. he was standing in front of the little cabin. He had somehow made it. He felt like he was going to pass out, but with great concentration and effort, he managed to get a fire going in the stove. He rolled out his sleeping bag and crawled in. Blackness.

Chapter Sixteen
Regroup

The 12th day came and went, and David hardly stirred. He had no bowel movement and didn't even get up to pee. When he woke, it was only for a short time and he would fall back to sleep. The fire had gone out, but there was no energy left to go out and collect more wood. On day thirteen he got up and went to the stream to drink and then crawled back into the sleeping bag. That night in the freezing cold he began to hallucinate. He tossed and turned, and he had muscle spasms in his legs. The cut on his forehead crusted over. He felt filthy. He was filthy. He was starving. He was weak. He felt like he was losing his mind and found it hard to think clearly. He knew that he was losing the battle to survive. All those survival books that he read, all the shows on survival he watched hadn't done him any good yet. He was lost and he had very little equipment to work with. He forced himself to get out of bed and get himself down to the stream and drink. He decided to dig around in the rubbish around the cabin to try and find another bottle or something he could carry water in. Everything was frozen and covered in snow, so it was not easy. Three quarters of an hour later, he tore a plastic bag open and found three plastic Pepsi bottles. They were one litre bottles, two with lids still screwed on. This was a life saver. With little strength he had, he made his way down again to the little stream. Using his buck knife, he opened a hole in the ice big enough to submerge the bottles. He rinsed them each three times and then filled them. He found he couldn't carry all three at once, so he had to make two trips back to the cabin. One bottle in each hand the first time and the one without a cap the second time. He was spent by the time he finished this task, but he had 3 litres of water. The fire was out, and he had no more wood. There was no way he could go out again to get wood, so he just crawled into his sleeping bag. The cabin was pretty cold, but at least he was sheltered from the wind and he had a good sleeping bag, which he covered with his parka. He took a long drink and fell back to sleep.

Chapter Seventeen
The search is on.

Lorenda called Harley on the morning of Nov 25th. "Harley, your dad told me he would be home no later than the 24th and I haven't heard from him."

"Mom, I wouldn't worry too much. We've had a fair bit of snow since dad has left. He may be having trouble getting himself out of the bush. If we don't hear from him in a couple days, we'll go look for him. Don't worry, he knows his way around up there. He'll be alright."

Lorenda had very mixed feelings. What had she done? Her plan had probably worked. David was more than likely lying dead up in Pete's cabin. She was genuinely feeling very panicky and so shitty about herself. How could have she done this? She really had no love left for David, but murder? What the hell was she thinking. He wasn't that horrible. She could have just left. She would wait another day and then send the boys up to find him. They would have to get some snowmobiles and supplies together. She called her son Rick. Should they call the police?

"No mom, don't panic. Dad has spent a lot of time in the bush. He's been there several times before. He will likely show up in a day or two. " Do you remember the time that he was up hunting with Pete, and they got that huge wet snowfall? It bent over all the trees across the trail and it took them two full days with the chain saw to cut all the trails out. Let's wait a bit."

Lorenda knew that wasn't the case here, but of course she couldn't say anything. She was biting her nails to the quick. Two days past. Harley and Rick made preparations. They borrowed a truck and two snowmobiles from friends. Harley had contacted

Pete and got specific directions on how to get into his cabin. They also got the GPS coordinates. Rick contacted the Police and the game warden in Prescott, the nearest big town to Pete's cabin. No one had seen or heard from David, but the game warden agreed to accompany Rick and Harley into the cabin. The game warden knew where the cabin was, although he hadn't been there for a couple years. He had even met David before, and thought he remembered checking his hunting license one time.

The Warden was Cliff Black, a tall, muscular man that no one in the area liked very much. He had a reputation of being mean, intolerant, and went strictly by the book. He was thirty-eight and he had been the warden in Prescott for nine years.

Harley and Rick met warden Black in Lovely. They had been up at 5 and got an early start in order to get into the cabin the same day. They met Black at the local Chinese restaurant and had coffee. Cliff asked them when David had gone in, details of how long he was going to stay, what he was driving and other pertinent information. If they didn't find David for some reason, they could report him as a missing person. The Warden predicted that possibly David could have been injured or something like that was causing the delay. They all knew there was no cell service in that part of the country, so it wasn't too unusual that they hadn't heard from him.

The warden led the way. Both trucks were four- wheel drives and although they already had a lot of snow this year, they had no trouble getting to the turn off into the bush trail that led to the cabin. Here they unloaded the snow machines. They took a couple thermoses of hot coffee, some water and sandwiches in a pack sack.

No one had driven or snowmobiled in on this trail. There were no tracks anywhere. No footprints, no quad tracks. No hunters had been this way. The moose season didn't open for another week. They followed the trail to where it met the river. Warden Black informed the boys that there once was an old log bridge here. It was washed out by the ice a couple of years back. They stopped here for a break. The warden suggested that they leave the trail and follow the river in from here. They had no idea that the truck they were looking for was just a few yards away, under the frozen ice and completely hidden by 2 feet of snow. They surmised the truck should have been left here, had David come this way, as he couldn't cross the river. Harley suggested, maybe if the ice was frozen when he arrived, he could have driven across.

"Impossible" said the warden.

"The banks are much too steep"

At any rate there were absolutely no signs that anyone had been here recently.

They started off through the deep snow. Warden Black leading the way. In a little over an hour, they were in the vicinity of the cabin. The warden had stopped a few times to see if he could find the way up to the cabin. It was built high up on a ridge and back from the riverbank, so it was not visible from the river. In addition to this, most every year when the ice went out in the spring - time, it scraped the river- banks clean. This obliterated any walking trails up, so it made it difficult to discern where exactly to go up the bank. The banks here were quite steep, and they didn't think they could go up with the snowmobiles. It was rugged territory and there was lots of willow brush to get through as well.

Cliff held up his hand to signal a stop and shut off his machine. Luckily the boys had got the GPS co-ordinates from Pete. They had a coffee to warm up. The warden punched the co-ordinates into his GPS. They were close, maybe three quarters of a mile. There were no man tracks anywhere. They drove on a bit farther and then stopped and made their way to the top of the bank on foot. It was hard work, picking their way through the bush and trudging through the deep snow. Near the top of the bank, they spotted the trail; and they could make out the chimney of the cabin. In 5 minutes, they stood in front of the log cabin.

It was an impressive structure considering the location. Log walls with a metal roof. Two large windows in the front and two smaller windows on the westside. The windows were boarded up. This was a common practice to keep out the bears. There was a small deck in the front with an overhang from the roof covering the deck. Hanging on the walls were several lengths of chains, ropes and wires. There were also some pails, a wood table and an old rocking chair on the deck. It had been built by hand using chain saws to cut and shape the logs. There was a snow drift across the front door. No tracks anywhere.

"Your dad hasn't been here. There are no signs that anyone has been here for a long time.

Certainly not this year."

Pete had told them where to find a key for the door. It only took a minute for Rick to locate it. Even with the door open, it was dark inside. The warden looked in with his flashlight. He swept the light from side to side. They could see mouse droppings on the counter tops, the table, and the window - sills. Spider webs were in the corners, on the ceiling; and hung from the wood stove. The cabin smelled musty and dank. It was obvious no one had been there or stayed there recently They retreated outside and discussed what they had found. David hadn't been there at all. He must have used this premise to get away and most likely had been somewhere else all this time. Warden Black asked:

"Has your dad been depressed or had any mental health issues? Is he a heavy drinker?" Rick and Harley assured him neither had been the case.

The wind was whipping up and it once again started to snow. Once the cabin was locked up, the trio made their way back to the snowmobiles. It was time to head back if they were to get back to the vehicles and out to the road before dark. It looked like another snowstorm was rolling in. The locals were already calling it the year of the big snow.

Back in Prescott, Harley and Rick got a hotel room. They phoned Lorrenda and their wives to relate what had transpired that day. The boys were dumfounded. It was not like David to just run off somewhere. Why would he? He had a good life, a good wife. He had money, a successful business. Was there some dark secret they were not aware of?

Harley asked his mom

"Were you and dad getting along okay?"

Lorenda's voice was shaky.

"Yes, we were fine. You know Harley, that we always had our differences and of course some small arguments, but nothing that would make him run off like this."

"Will you look around on other roads in the area?" asked Lorenda.

"Yes, Rick and I will go to the police station in the morning and file a report. You should do the same thing mom. Then we're going to get some maps of the area and search for Rick's truck. I'm going to see if the police will do an aerial search in the vicinity of Pete's cabin."

Lorenda sat back in her lounge chair with a large Gin and tonic in her hand. What could have happened to David? Where was the truck? Why had he not gone to the cabin? Could he have possibly known the scheme she had concocted? Endless questions and scenarios were going around and around in her mind. Perhaps he had taken an Excedrin before he got there, but it didn't kill him. Nothing made much sense. She drank until she couldn't stay awake any longer and in a drunken stupor stumbled up the stairs to bed.

Chapter Eighteen
Police Report

The next morning, she got herself together and went to the Police station to report her husband missing. She didn't have to act upset; she was. Corporal Diego took her statement and passed it on to her superior. Lorenda was asked to come into an interrogation room. Detective Sergeant Mike Kane, a twenty-year veteran on the force, spent the next two hours asking Lorenda questions. He was gentle with her and sympathetic. He felt her reactions to the situation were genuine. She was really shaken, but not hysterical. Naturally when someone goes missing, the first place the police look for answers are at the spouse, and nearest of kin. At this point they had no reason to suspect a homicide. It was a case of a missing person. Enough time had lapsed that they would act upon it immediately. A missing person bulletin would be put out. Posters would be made up and distributed. An aerial search around the cabin area would be conducted. A description of Rick's Toyota Tundra and license number would be put out to all police personnel. The authorities would begin to question people in hotels, gas stations, and restaurants around Prescott, Lovely and the surrounding district. David had been gone or missing now for nineteen days. Detective Kane thought to himself, David was probably in Vegas or somewhere with a new girlfriend. They'd seen this type of thing happen many times before. Midlife crisis. They would do an initial investigation and search, but not go too much further with this until something surfaced.

Nov 30th.

The following morning was sunny and calm. It had snowed and drifted throughout the night. The RCMP sent out a light plane to scour the area of Pete's cabin. Only the most recent animal tracks were visible in the snow. Once more, the fresh snow had erased all. They could detect no tracks, human or from vehicles in that immediate area. No abandoned vehicles. Not a single clue to follow up on. After an hour, the plane returned to Prescott. That would be the end of the aerial search. Too expensive and not enough to go on. Rick and Harley drove up and down the main roads and drove in where they could on side roads. They quickly realized that this was an effort in futility. They were searching for a needle in a hay - stack and they would need an army to check out all these little side roads and trails in the area. Regardless, they spent the day searching for the truck and talking to whomever they could along the way, asking if anyone had seen a Grey Toyota Tundra or their dad. They stopped at grocery stores, little bars, gas stations and farm- yards. No one had seen anything. Rick and Harley were beginning to think there was something more to this mystery. David had probably not come to this area at all. The next morning, they returned home.

Lorenda spent the next several days with Harley and Janice. She didn't want to be by herself. They along with Rick and his wife Mattie discussed what should be done. So far none of the people the police had questioned remembered seeing David or the Toyota truck.

Secretly, Lorenda was losing it. She could not for the life of her, figure out what might have happened. People simply don't disappear. Logically David could not have known what she had done. Things just didn't add up. She didn't know if one of these mornings, David would walk through the door or if the police would find his body and suspect she had something to do with his death. She was a nervous wreck.

Chapter Nineteen
Go or Stay

David woke up late morning. He was very thirsty, but his head had cleared somewhat. He still felt groggy, tired and was extremely hungry. He guessed he had probably lost twenty-five or thirty pounds. It was freezing cold in the little shelter. If he was going to dig himself out of this mess, one of two things had to happen soon. He needed to get a fire going and he needed to get something into his stomach. He filled his belly with water. Got up and put on his parka. It would be great to have some gloves, to gather wood, but he would just have to suck it up. He went out and slowly set himself to his task. He gathered smaller dead branches; a couple arm loads. He methodically broke them up and cleaned out the airtight stove. He found the lighter in his pocket and soon had a small fire going. Adding a half dozen bigger sticks and he could soon feel some heat coming out of the airtight. That was the beauty of an airtight stove. They heated up really quick. He went out again several times and brought in bigger branches breaking them into lengths that would fit into the stove. In forty-five minutes, the cabin again was toasty warm. Had he got the fire going the day before, the search plane would most likely have seen it. He had dreamed he heard a plane, was it yesterday or the day before? He hadn't been out of bed for two days, except briefly to go out and get water or to pee. In a few hours with the warmth of the shack, David began to feel a little bit better. He began to think of how he could get food. He had no wire for snares, no bait, no weapons except the homemade spear and his buck knife. His best bet was finding a grouse and killing it or using the box trap to catch another fisher or whatever he could lure in.

He came up with a logical plan. At least he thought it was logical. There were mice in the cabin. He hadn't seen any lately, but he had heard them scurrying about in the dark. If he could kill a mouse, he would cut it open and use it for bait as he had before in the coke box set. Then he would fashion a throwing stick, kind of like a boomerang. A piece of wood perhaps eighteen inches long and as big around as his wrist. If he got close enough to a grouse, he may be able to stun it with this and then kill it with his spear or knife. Pretty crude, but that's all he could come up with. He was finding it hard to move around so he planned to do this in order.

He sat with club in hand for 2 hours before he saw a mouse come out of a corner and begin to gnaw on the corner of his sleeping bag. He didn't even have to get up. Whack, he had it! He had killed his mouse. His emotions were running high. Tears came to his eyes. First step completed. The coke box was outside. He got some thread from his shirt to tie the mouse to the underside of the box. He wanted to make sure that whatever was going to try to get it, it would not get it easily and hopefully would trip the set to close the box and trap the animal. If it were a large animal like a fox or a wolf, the trap would be too small. However, there were lots of smaller animals that would fit under, like a marten, a small fisher, a weasel, maybe a skunk. Who knows what might go for the bait.

On the way back to the cabin, he gathered more sticks for the fire. While doing this he noticed rabbit tracks. His heart was racing. He took the firewood back and got the spear and his throwing stick. He had limited energy, so he moved slowly. That actually was good anyway. When you're hunting you should move slowly. He followed the tracks. Of course, the stupid rabbit wouldn't follow the trail. He had to go into the thicker brush. A squirrel chirped loudly in a nearby tree. It was their way to warn of danger. David found it hard to keep his hands warm while carrying the two weapons. This was something he would have to find a solution to. Every 10 minutes he would have to stop and put his hands up his sleeves or under his arms to warm them a bit. It was getting dark and he would have to make his way back soon.

Suddenly a bush chicken flew up in front of him. It startled him and he nearly fell backward. The grouse only went about 8 ft and landed in a small spruce tree. David composed himself and very slowly advanced a couple steps and then threw the throwing stick. He knocked the grouse out of the tree, but it was not dead. It was wounded and tried to get itself under some brush. David hurried toward it and tried to hit it with the point of his spear. The spear glanced off, but on his second attempt, it went into the grouse's body.

David was panting. He was spent, but he yelled at the top of his lungs. YES, YES, YES! He was going to eat tonight. He gathered up the grouse, his spear, and throwing stick. Slowly he made his way back to the cabin. It was dark by the time he got there. By the light of the fire, he gutted the bird. Now should he eat all of it at once? He decided to cook it all on top the airtight, but to save 1/3 until he got more to eat. The lid on the airtight was rusty and dirty, but David really had nothing to clean it with. He simply set the meat on the metal stove top and turned it over until it was cooked. When it was done, he did his best to scrape the dirt and rust off the meat with his buck knife. Even without any spices or condiments it tasted heavenly. When you are starving, any food is welcomed.

He didn't really feel full, but much better. It settles the mind when you have food in your tummy. He saved the bones in a little pile on the table. He lay in his bed thinking that maybe it was best was to stay put for a while. Right now, he couldn't walk any long distances anyway. He was too weak. It was apparent that there was game in the vicinity. Hopefully in one location, he could obtain more to eat and regain his strength. Perhaps, he would be rescued. When he didn't return home, Lorenda and the boys would certainly come looking. They had known where he was going. It shouldn't be that difficult. He was unsure if the top of the truck cab was above or below the waterline. If they came looking, and it was sticking out above the water, certainly he would be rescued.

Once again, David took stock of his situation. How could he increase his odds of survival? This was no TV show or game now. What plan he came up with could mean life or death. It gave him some hope to just make a mental list. 1- It was warm inside his shelter and he could even improve on that. He could fill in the gaps that still existed where he had patched the hole in the roof. In addition, he could chink between the logs to make the cabin a little more airtight .2- He could search out a clearing and make an S.O.S sign that might be spotted from the air. Not many planes had flown over and none of them close, but it was worth a shot. 3- If he was diligent, he may even get a cache of food stored up to travel with. Right now, in his condition, he could not travel far. He had to focus on building his strength up. A pot or some sort of vessel to boil water in would be an enormous boost. Tea could then be made from pine needles and he could boil the bones of the birds to make a soup or broth. He would spend more time digging through the trash pile outside. 4 – He would try to fashion some type of mitts for his hands, possibly from the fisher pelt. That would be a huge improvement as well. It was very difficult to keep his hands warm when out walking, especially when carrying his gear.

Chapter Twenty
Settling in Nov 24th

It felt good to settle in. He was going to free his mind from the worry and stress of finding Pete's cabin for now. It drove him crazy trying to figure out how he could be so lost. It was a real mystery that he hadn't run into the Beacon river. He must be really off track somehow. Perhaps after coming out of the river, in shock, he must have started off in the wrong direction. Perhaps he was making big circles. He had read, that this is quite common. People lost in the bush think they are going in a straight line, but really, they gradually go right or left as they walk.

They eventually will go in a complete circle. He had walked for many days. He may be too far north. He could be 10 or even Twenty miles too far north. He had no idea. A real puzzle, but he was not going to worry about it for now. He knew he didn't want to spend another night out in the bush with no protection. It was no doubt going to get colder and he had made one big mistake already that nearly cooked him. He could not afford to make another.

The morning was bright. The birds were singing. He could hear squirrels chirping in the distance. First task was to fill the water jugs. He thought of how lucky he had been to find this overnight camp. Without it he was sure he would be dead. Next, he spent 3 hours gathering wood and breaking branches for his stove. He stacked as much as he could inside the cabin and made a pile outside as well. He walked over and checked his box trap. Nothing had disturbed it.

At noon he ate the rest of the grouse. He sipped water constantly to keep from getting dehydrated and it felt good to keep his stomach full, even if it was just water.

He brought out the Fisher skin, and with his jack knife, he carved out 4 pieces that would cover both sides of his hands. With the point of his knife, he made small slits around the outer edges. He then cut some thin strips from the hide in order that he could thread them through the slits he had made. By mid- afternoon, he had a very crude pair of mitts. The fur facing the inside. He tried them on and low and behold, he thought they would do just fine. Certainly, better than nothing.

Alright, one mission accomplished. He was already played out, but he thought he would try a hunting walk. Half hour out, half hour back. It was a pretty mild day with virtually no wind. He took his spear and throwing stick and ventured out. He saw birds in the trees. He also saw a couple of squirrels, but he knew there was no chance of hitting those with a throw. They were much too fast, and he didn't want to expend any energy unnecessarily. He veered off on a little game trail that he hadn't been on before. There were rabbit tracks in the snow. He sure wished he had some wire to set a snare. He knew how to snare rabbits and to snare squirrels as well. He was just about to turn back when he saw some other tracks. They were wolf tracks and they looked pretty fresh. His eyes scoured the perimeter. Suddenly, David was on high alert. He didn't think wolves would normally attack a human, but if they were hungry enough, they would. He walked around a bit studying the tracks. He thought there were perhaps two of them. It was good that there were not more. He found a kill site, where they had got a rabbit. There was a little blood in the snow and a bit of fur. Nothing else remained. He turned around and retraced his steps, slowly making his way back to the cabin. That unnerved him.

The fire was out when he returned. He broke up some little branches to start the fire and when he went to light it, the lighter would not work. He flicked the wheel many times. Shook it, tried again. No more fuel in that one. He got his second lighter and re-lit the stove. Oh shit, this was not a good day. If and when the second lighter went dry, he would be forced to strike out to find Pete's cabin or never let the fire go out in this one. David did not sleep well that night. He was shaken to the core. He got up every half hour or forty- five minutes to re-stoke the fire, just to make sure it didn't go out. From now on, he would not use that lighter unless it was absolutely necessary. Throughout the night, he could hear the wolves howling. They were not too far away.

Nov 25th. Day 15 in the woods

In the morning, the next task he thought was a priority, was to look through the garbage heap for a pot. It was noticeably colder. He first replenished the wood he had burned the day before. He was glad to have the mitts. That was a big help. He used a sturdy stick to dig through the plastic bags, cans, old boards etc. He found an old metal coffee pot. The name Everwear was on the bottom. He couldn't find a lid, but this was a real find. He hurried down to the stream and washed it out the best he could. Luckily for him the little creek had some open water under some brush and snow, where it went down a small water fall maybe 10 inches high. Each time he went for water, it was open water. If it was frozen over, he could easily break through the ice with his buck knife. David was excited. This was a game changer. He went up to the shack and restoked the fire. He set the coffee pot on the lid of the airtight and then went out to gather some pine needles. Once the water was boiling, he threw in a handful of pine needles and then some of the bigger grouse bones. He let it all simmer for around 20 minutes. Then one by one, he took out the bones, let them cool a bit, and broke them open with a stone and his buck knife. He sucked the marrow out of the bones, which he found delicious. He then cooled the liquid and drank it. It tasted like shit, but it was hot. That's something he hadn't had for weeks. A hot drink! He refilled the coffee pot and placed the remaining bones from the grouse in it. That would be his next "tea". He lay down for a little rest. He was exhausted from the morning's activity. As he dozed off, he thought of Lorenda, the boys and the grandkids. He missed them tremendously. Why were they not here looking for him? They must know something is wrong by now. It was like living in a very bad dream. Nothing made any sense. He dozed off. The hot liquid in his belly felt so great. He had forgotten how it felt to be warmed from the inside. Two hours later, he woke up. The fire was nearly out, but there were hot coals still. He rekindled the fire. He drank some of his tea, then went out to check the box trap. The box was on the ground, but there was nothing inside. The mouse was gone. It looked to David like maybe a marten track around the box. He was disappointed, but encouraged because he at least had game coming to the set. He reset the trap. He had no bait, but he took what was left of the hides and a few bones and used that for bait to re- set the trap. He went back to sip tea and see if he could catch another mouse. He didn't have the energy to go on a hunting walk and it would be dark in a couple hours. Every half hour or so he would go out and push snow and pine branches in between the logs, to chink them up. It didn't work very well. He got more green branches and threw them on the roof to cover over the hole and just for insulation in general.

The work kept his mind occupied and it felt good to be improving his lot, even a little.

He heard another plane in the distance. A small plane. There were always jets going over every day, but they were at 30,000 ft .Obviously that was of no use. That night the wolves were howling again. It made him very nervous.

Chapter Twenty-one
Back at the ranch...

Lorenda was talking strategy with her boys and their wives. She asked, "Should we be hiring our own plane to do another search in the area around Pete's cabin?" Rick said "Well, that wouldn't make sense, because there is absolutely no sign that he even went in there. I think that would be a waste of time and money".

Matti interjected,

"We have to get records of him using credit cards or something to find out where he went."

Harley said,

"He must not want us to find him or he would have contacted us. I have a feeling he's not in any danger. No 911 call, no contact. It's hard to know what it all means." "If he's not in the bush, his phone should be working."

Lorenda told them she had tried calling several times. They all had tried many times. Rick volunteered to call the phone carrier to see if there had been any activity. Harley said he would call Visa and Mastercard to see if there had been any purchases made. The police were not getting anywhere, but it seemed they were not trying very hard.

Christmas parties were in full swing. With David missing, Lorenda contacted the manager at Smith's lock and key. She knew Greg had been the manager for several years now and was very capable of running the company. To keep up a façade, she asked Greg if David had indicated anything to him, before he left, that might explain his disappearance. He assured her that nothing seemed out of the ordinary when he left. Lorenda had very little to do with the business over the years, but she was the wife, so she told Greg to arrange for the company Christmas party. She said, "Just carry on as if the business was your own. We'll make sure your well compensated." Rick and Harley had helped out at the shop lots of times over the years, but they had no idea of how to run it. Lorenda didn't want them to get involved or start handling any of the cash. Both of them had trouble managing their own household finances. Harley would just gamble it away if he got the opportunity.

Chapter Twenty-Two
Trying to survive

It was Nov 26th. David had to light the fire again this morning. It had gone out. Rats, he hated now to use the lighter. He boiled some water and had a hot drink. No cup to put it in, had to drink from the pot. That required him to wait until it cooled somewhat. Quite a process just to have a drink of hot water, but it was worth it. He stoked the airtight and went out to check his box trap. Nothing had moved and he didn't see any new tracks. He retreated to the little cabin and got his spear and throwing stick. He took a long drink of water. He wasn't going to be taking any along. It was too heavy. He replenished the water and the firewood and then struck out.

The day was overcast. A cold wind was blowing. The bush seemed silent except for the wind and the trees brushing together. If he tucked the spear and throwing stick under his arms and kept his mitts in his Parka pockets, he could keep his hands warm. His Parka was a good one, but his legs would often get cold if there was wind. He had on some long johns, but they didn't do the trick on a day like today. He was weak and the walking was tuff, but he absolutely had to kill something to eat or he wouldn't last much longer. He knew the odds were stacked against him. He thought about his scent. It was likely stronger than a man's normally would be. He hadn't washed for over two weeks, only his hands in the stream and occasionally, his face. He, of course had no toilet paper. He had been wiping with his hand and then rubbing it on the snow or on spruce branches. He could only imagine what he smelled like. He had to move slowly or he was soon panting. Once again, it began to snow. He went along without seeing much.

The odd bird flitting around. The odd squirrel. An hour passed and then two. The snow was getting heavier now. He came to an embankment. It looked like maybe an old river bed. It was fairly devoid of trees in the bottom. A movement caught his eye down there. He watched closely. It was a wolf. In another moment he saw another and then a third. He was downwind of them, so they hadn't detected him. He crouched down and watched. His heart thumping wildly.

There were five in all. They didn't seem to be travelling, just sort of milling around. Lying down, then getting up and circling about as if looking for something. Perhaps hunting mice. Most people don't know it but a large part of a wolf's diet is mice. They usually travel in Packs. The pack is usually led by a female. An alfa wolf. They have a territory which they mark by peeing. When hunting they can travel up to 60 miles a day. Their range is huge. It often takes them a week to make a circuit. They keep going over the same territory, very often using the same trails. They mainly live on small rodents and often follow deer, elk, and moose watching for one that is injured or showing signs of sickness. When they find one, they work together to bring it down.

David was scarred shitless. He slowly backed away, retracing his steps. He wanted to run, but fought back the urge. He didn't want to make any noise and he knew in his condition, if he ran, it wouldn't be long before he collapsed anyway. He followed his tracks back as they were filling with the fresh snow. Again, a movement in the corner of his eye. A sharp tail grouse. It was just sitting, just huddled against a fallen log. He got his throwing stick ready and moved slowly ahead. When it went to fly, he threw. He hit it, but the bird went under some brush. David had seen where it went in. As he approached the grouse scurried another 6 ft away. David followed. Again, the bird found some cover. David could tell it was injured and he wasn't going to lose this meal. He approached again, this time getting a little closer. He threw his spear, missed. The bird ran off again, another 6 or 8 ft. David running behind, threw the throwing stick at it. Bingo, another hit and the bird lay still. He ran up and grabbed it and cut off it's head with his buck knife. He was out of wind, completely exhausted, but he was elated. He decided that he would gut it at home as he wanted to save the guts for bait.

It was snowing quite heavily. David gathered his throwing stick and the spear. Off he went with his prize. There was new spring in his step. He felt elated. Food! He wanted to get back to the little cabin and cook this feast up. It took another hour to get home. He cleaned the grouse, gathered more firewood and had to re- light his fire as it had gone out. Then he cooked it up on the stove top. Oh, how delicious it tasted. It took will power to only eat half. He saved the rest for tomorrow. A candle would sure be nice. If he lifted the lid on the airtight, it gave out a little glow from the fire. He couldn't open it too much or it would smoke up the shack. He went to sleep thinking of his family and how much he missed them all, even Lorenda.

Chapter Twenty-three
Suspicions Dec 4th

Lorenda and the boys met for lunch on Tuesday at Boston Pizza. Lorenda liked the food there but felt it was just a wee bit pricey. Harley and Rick both ordered steins of beer with their pizza. Lorenda ordered Greek salad had a glass of red wine with hers.

Harley had called Visa. He had a hard time convincing them to give him any information but the lady he was talking with finally gave in. The last entry on David's card was in Lovely for gas. It was on Nov 10th. No charges on the card after that. Rick had called Rodgers about the phone records, but they wouldn't tell him anything, however they agreed to give Mike Kane a call. In turn Detective Kane called Rick back. There were no calls made from David's phone after Nov 9th. It appeared to the trio that David was going to the cabin, but somehow never made it there. It was mind boggling. Where could he have gone and why?

Rick was highly suspicious.

"Mom, do you think dad met someone? Have you ever been suspicious of him cheating on you?"

"I don't think so. There's never been any reason to suspect him. It's just not in his nature."

Harley asked, "Have you checked on his bank account mom? You guys have a joint account. Is there money missing? Any withdrawals after he left?"

Rick chirped in.

"What's happening with the business account? Are you on that account or just dad?"

"No, my name is on all of the accounts, and I've already checked that out. He hasn't withdrawn a dime."

Lorenda told them she had a very good friend that worked at the bank. She would ask her to check if David maybe had an account they weren't aware of, or maybe he had been squirreling money away in a safe deposit box. Of course, secretly she knew that none of this was very likely, but she really didn't know what was going on anymore. Where had he gone?

Driving home, Harley started thinking that if his dad didn't surface, that maybe he would be in for an inheritance. He didn't know what his mom and dad were worth, but he knew that they had a fair bit. He guessed like maybe eight hundred thousand, a million? The business must be worth that much as well. He thought he should find out if his dad had a will. Was everything left to Lorenda or were he and Rick in the will as well? He chastised himself for thinking like that, but he couldn't help it. He started fantasizing of what he could do if he came into a lot of money. There would be extravagant trips to Vegas. At least one. He often thought of what it would be like to be a high roller. Janice would be staying home for that one. Harley loved Roulette. It would be thrilling to start with a bank roll of a thousand or two. Then he would show them he was a winner. He had been playing the VLT's way too much lately. There were several unpaid bills and he had borrowed almost $3000.00 from 3 friends over the past 4 months. None of them would lend him anymore money. It would be great to get his hands on some money. He would ask his mom about the will, but he didn't know how to go about it without making himself look bad.

Mike Kane had let some time pass to see if David would resurface. He decided he would take another look at the case. Two days ago, Rodgers had called him regarding David's cell phone records and he in turn had called David's son Rick with the results. Harley had also called him and reported that David had not used his Visa since Nov 9th. The detective felt a bit guilty that David's family were apparently starting their own investigation, so he figured he would give it some of his time. He picked up the phone and scheduled interviews with Lorenda, Rick and Harley. When someone vanishes, the place to look first is the immediate family. Most often there is foul play involved.

His first interview was with Lorenda. Detective Kane had phoned her and asked if she would like to come into the station or if she preferred, he could come to her house. Lorenda thought it would be more comfortable in her home. Corporal Diego accompanied Kane when they went to the interview. It was an older two storey home, but very well kept. Once inside the detective could see the home was spotlessly clean. She invited them into the living room and had tea already made. Diego informed her that they would be recording the interview and asked if she was okay with that. Lorenda indicated that was no problem. Both he and Kane noticed she seemed quite nervous.

"Mrs. Smith, When did you first meet your husband?"

"We met in high school. Really we've been together our whole adult lives."

"And how many years have you been married?"

"Twenty - six years, it will be twenty- seven come this summer."

"Would you say that you and David have a good marriage"

Lorenda squirmed in her chair a little and looked down.

"Yes, it's always been pretty good. We've had some ups and downs like everyone else, but hey we're 26 years together, so that should tell you something."

"Was there ever any infidelity?"

"No, never."

"Are you sure?"

"I'm sure."

"How is David's relationship with his sons?"

"It's good. They all get along well."

"How about your neighbours? Get along well with them?"

"We don't socialize too much with our neighbours. We know them and talk to them occasionally, but we don't get together socially with any of them."

"No disputes with them about anything?"

"No. none whatsoever."

"Okay, how about at work. Does your husband get along well with everyone there?"

"I think so, I'm really not too involved with David's work."

"Has he fired anyone recently that may have a grudge?"

"Not to my knowledge. You could check with Greg our manager at the shop."

"I'll do that. I'm sorry but I have to ask some uncomfortable questions. Have you taken out any new life insurance policies in the past year or two?"

"No, not at all."

"Changed anything on existing policies"

"No, not to my knowledge."

"Have you been involved with anyone besides your husband in the past year or two?"

"No, absolutely not. I'm quite sure David has not been either."

"Can you think of anyone at all, that may want to harm your husband?"

"No, believe me, I've thought about that. David was a pretty easy- going person. Everyone liked him."

"Was?"

"I meant is. He is a pretty easy- going person."

"Do you have any ideas on where David could be or where he may have gone?"

"No, I have no idea. It's certainly not like him to just run off or disappear. He's never done that before."

"Has David ever shown any signs of Dementia or Alzimers?"

"No, not at all."

"Alright, does David have sibblings?"

"Yes, three brothers. David is the youngest. They aren't super close, but they never really fight or anything."

This line of questioning went on for some time.

"Okay Mrs. Smith. Thank you for your time, and thanks for the tea. We'll keep you informed if anything develops. Please call anytime if you think of anything else that may help us find your husband."

Back in the car Kane asked Diego what she thought?

"Was she keeping anything from us?"

Diego said, "I have a feeling there is something. She seemed very nervous. Did you see how she kept fidgeting and wringing her hands?"

"Yes, but her husband is missing, I think that might be normal."

"Hard to say. Something seemed off to me."

"You could be right, I sensed that as well."

In the following days, detective Kane interviewed Harley, Rick, and Greg." He found nothing unusual. No leads to follow up on. He thought of all the possible scenarios. If he was up in the bush somewhere, possibly lost or dead, where was the truck? He would phone the game warden again, what was his name? He looked at his notes. Black, Cliff Black. He would ask Cliff to go have a closer look at the road in there. He wanted to make sure that truck wasn't on some side trail, maybe not visible from the main trails. That was the only thing that made any sense at this point. Maybe have another look around the cabin for any clues. Anything that might point them in the right direction.

Chapter Twenty-Four
No fuel

Dec 5th. David woke and he could hear something outside. It sounded like someone walking. He looked out the window but could see nothing. He got his parka and boots on and went outside. There was a moose about 40 yards down the trail. It had walked right by the cabin. It was a nice site, but really of no use to David. He couldn't kill a moose with his little homemade spear or throwing stick. The moose looked back over it's shoulder and then walked off, unconcerned. David noticed the temperature was considerably colder than the day before. He guessed it might be -20C or -25C . Much colder in the little cabin when he crawled out of bed. He got his water bottles and filled them at the stream. He gathered some spruce needles for tea. He left them on the branches and boiled them for about 30 minutes. This way when he pulled out the little branches, there were no needles left in the water. David was unsure if this was the way it was supposed to be done, but it didn't matter. It worked for him.

The little cabin heated up quickly because it was so small. He got the rest of the grouse and cooked it on the stove lid. Grouse and tea for breakfast. Better than most days. He then got the guts from the bird and went out to his coke box trap. Nothing in there, so he reset it using the entrails of the grouse. That should bring something in. Although it was nasty cold, he decided to go hunting as he had to eat.

The snow was about two feet deep or more. It made walking hard. His homemade mitts didn't help too much in this weather and his legs were cold too. He thought a lot while he was walking about the directions. He knew the sun rose in the east, set in the west, and was sure where north and south were in relation to the cabin. What he didn't know was where he was in relation to Pete's cabin. It could be in any direction from here. Logically he should be within a days walk of Pete's cabin. He was sure this shack had been used years ago as an out camp by a trapper. It was possible that it was an out camp on someone else's trapline. Not Pete's. No matter who's it was, there should be a main camp somewhere within an eight- or ten-mile radius. When he thought about that he realized it was a huge area to cover. He had to wait for a little warmer weather and then strike out again in search. His health was deteriorating and he couldn't last forever out here without some proper nutrition.

He noticed a poplar tree that had been ringed. About 8 feet off the ground, the bark had been eaten off in about a one- foot ring around the tree. He knew that this was a habit of porcupines. David looked around the bottom of the tree and found tracks. He did his best to follow them, watching intently for any movement in the trees. The way to kill a porcupine is to whack it across the back of the neck. Porcupines are super tough and it's almost impossible to spear them or hit them in the body to do any damage. Their quills and a very thick hide protect them well from any predators. The best way is to break their neck.

David followed the tracks for over an hour. No site of the animal. He was freezing up and he wanted to get back to restoke the fire before it went out completely. When he returned, the fire was out. Unfortunately, so was the fuel in his lighter. Fucked! Absolutely fucked. He got some kindling, some old man's beard that he had stored and set it on the ashes. Very gently he blew on the tinder bundle. Nothing, the coals and ashes were cold. He sat back and put his face in his hands. Completely defeated. How had he been so stupid, as to let that fire go out. He broke down and sobbed for a good twenty minutes. He had a hard time keeping it together. Now what? David knew this was likely the end of the line. His luck had run out. He made the tinder bundle be the best that he could and shook the lighter vigorously. He ran his thumb over the striker and it lit, just long enough to get a flame in the tinder bundle. Very carefully he brought the fire to life. Thank the lord, he was going to live another day and he would be warm once again tonight. There was never a time in his life when he felt more grateful. His body was shaking uncontrollably. That was a close one. He was okay for now but he must never let that fire go out again. David considered himself a bush man, but he never started a fire using friction or whatever. He didn't think he could do that. He vowed to himself to check on his fire every hour day and night. A very dark foreboding feeling came over him. This was a game changer. He spent the rest of the daylight hours collecting wood for his fire. Fire meant warmth and life.

During the night, he allowed himself very little sleep. He was paranoid about the fire going out. The next morning and throughout the whole day he was obsessed with going out and collecting dry branches that he could break up for firewood for his stove. The weather continued to get colder. It must be -30 now he thought. He amassed a huge stockpile of wood. He pretty much filled the little cabin with wood, although he left enough space to lay down to sleep. He also didn't put any too close to his stove for fear that a spark would jump and burn the cabin down while he slept. He checked the box trap once in the afternoon. Nothing there. The hunger was so consuming. It was on his mind night and day.

His hair was long. His beard was long. He was dirty, his clothes filthy. He was skinny, had probably lost 35 or 40 pounds. He had little stamina now, it was hard to move around, especially because of the freezing cold and the deep snow.

Next morning, he checked the box trap. He could hear something inside! He got a piece of wood that he could use as a club. He also took out his buck knife and stood his spear within an arms-length, on the nearest tree. He used the same method as he had done with the fisher. He lifted the box just a crack and immediately the animal tried to squeeze under. First the front paws came out and then the head. Once the head was through he knelt on top the box squeezing down on the neck. He then clubbed it in the head until there was no movement. He then took his knife and pushed it through the neck, just to make certain the animal was dead. He slowly lifted the box. It was a Marten. It had a beautiful brown pelt.

David dropped to his knees and cried. He was going to have lunch and supper today. He could stay warm. He could drink some type of soup broth from boiling the bones. He wasn't thriving, but he was staying alive. He was going to eat every morsel of this animal. Nothing would go to waste. He would eat the brains, suck the marrow from the bones, use the entrails for more bait in the box trap. He would dry the hide by the stove. He didn't have a toque. Maybe he could fashion some type of hat from it. If nothing else, he could lay on it for bedding.

As he cleaned the Marten, he was kind of in wonder that once the box trap had fallen on the animal, that it was unable to get out. Perhaps it was just heavy enough to keep the Marten prisoner. He had seen scratch marks in the ground where he thought it may have tried unsuccessfully to dig underneath. Whatever the case, it seemed the Marten had given up and just stayed still until David came. David had seen that more than once before, where an animal would be caught in a trap, maybe just by a toe or a paw and just remain there until it froze to death or the trapper came to claim it. On the other hand, he had seen where a fox or a coyote was caught by a leg and they would chew their own leg off to escape. At any rate, he was just happy and so grateful that he had caught it.

He cooked all of the meat and divided it into four meals. One portion he ate for lunch. Once the meat cooled, he cut it into bite sized cubes and strips. These he stored in his parka pockets. He figured he could make some containers from bark, to store the meat. That would be a little cleaner. He made a broth from boiling the bones and drank his fill that day and night. It was a joy to have something other than just plain water or boiled spruce needles. David did not particularly like the taste, but at least there was a taste. At supper time he ate a second portion. He was torn as to ration the meat over several days or eat it all in the next two days. He felt it necessary to build his strength, so he decided it would be just eaten at the next two meal times. Maybe he would be lucky enough to catch something else in the trap. He wouldn't hunt much, except for short excursions, because he was paranoid about leaving the fire go out and it was so fucking cold he wouldn't venture out too far anyway. Before dark he reset the box trap.

Chapter Twenty-Five
Doubts

It was Dec 6th. Almost a month since David had left. Lorenda was very jumpy. She was thinking, the police were suspecting, that she had something to do with David's disappearance. The questions they asked about infidelity and insurance policies had really rattled her. Every time the doorbell rang, or the phone rang, she nearly jumped out of her skin. Without knowing it, she was picking at her face. Scratching any little bump.

Could that detective Kane possibly know anything about the cyanide? She didn't think so, but the police could be very crafty when investigating like this. She had seen it on T.V. dozens of times. Harley and Rick even seemed suspicious. They had asked her questions that she didn't like.

She imagined that maybe David had found out about the cyanide. Perhaps he was now plotting to kill her in revenge. Perhaps that's why they couldn't find the truck or David. He was laying low somewhere near. The truck hidden in some underground garage or something. Maybe David was stalking her, just waiting for his chance to strike.

She stood looking out the front window. A man walked by on the other side of the street. Was that him? She couldn't see his face because his hood was up. It looked like David's build. He walked to the corner, turned to the right and soon was out of sight. Shit, that may have been him. She went to the kitchen and poured a large gin and tonic. Lorenda went back to the front window and stared out while she drank the gin. She was shaking.

A second gin, and she went from window to window, looking out to the back yard, the side yard, the front yard. Nothing.

The phone rang. She could see on the call display that it was from the city police. She ran up to her bedroom without answering. She let it ring until it stopped. They were on to her. What was she going to do? What if they asked her to take a lie detector? She wondered if she should be contacting a lawyer? No, that would make her look guilty.

She went back down to the kitchen, got the bottle of gin and one of tonic. She made sure the front and back doors were locked. Back in her bedroom, she locked the door behind her. She pulled a chair close to the window and poured another drink. Looking out in a daze, she thought she had better come up with some sort of a plan. She was picking at her face. David was on to her and she knew it. Should she go to detective Kane and tell him what she knew?

By 3 P.M. Lorenda was quite drunk. She took off her clothes and crawled under the covers and passed out. Several places on her face had droplets of blood oozing out from the scratching. The phone rang again. She didn't hear it. It rang several more times throughout the afternoon and evening. Lorenda heard it a couple of times, but did not answer. She got up once to pee and at the same time finished off the bottle of gin. She blacked out.

Chapter Twenty-Six
A second Look

Cliff Black had been asked to go take a second look at the road into Pete's cabin. He would also take a closer look in the area around the cabin to see if he could find any tracks or signs of David. He packed a lunch, and left early in the morning. At the turnoff into the bush, he unloaded the ski doo. It was cold, -28C. He had really good gear. Heated ski-doo suit, heated helmet and hand warmers. He drove slowly looking for any signs. Any trails running off the main trail were checked out. It was a bit unusual that there were no hunters that had come into this area this year. There was not one quad or ski-doo track. He made his way slowly to where the trail met the Beacon river. He went down the embankment to the river and stopped in the middle on the ice. He knew that the homemade bridge here had been washed out a couple of years ago. Anyone coming in this way, would have to carry on by foot or by snow machine. He had been informed by David's family, that David did not have a sled along. It was apparent to him that David had not been here.

He took out his knap sack and poured a hot coffee from his thermos. The chicken salad sandwich was not frozen yet and he was enjoying his lunch. He scoured the surrounding area while he sat there, looking for something, anything. Little did he know that the truck was a few yards downstream from him hidden under the ice and snow.

It didn't make much sense to him, but after he finished his lunch he followed the river down towards Pete's cabin. He drove slowly, because it was so cold and because he was looking for any signs that David may have come this way. He was careful to watch out for any creeks that may be flowing into the river. He was somewhat familiar with the area and knew the two major creeks, Bailey creek and Wolf Creek dumped into the river somewhere before he reached Pete's cabin. At these points he would stay in the middle of the river and speed up. The ice can be thin where there is any rapidly moving water, even in the dead of winter. In the years he was a game warden, he had seen several incidents where skidoos had gone through the ice.

When he reached Pete's cabin, he left his sled on the river and walked up the bank to the cabin. He found the key and once again looked through the interior. Nothing had been touched. He walked around the little clearing around the cabin. He sat on a log for about half hour and just listened. Other than the birds and squirrels, there was no sound. He decided to follow the river downstream for a couple miles to look for any human tracks, or tracks from any machines. Except for animal tracks, the snow was pristine.

Cliff turned his sled around and headed back to his truck and town. He felt certain David was not in this area and likely never had been.

Chapter Twenty-Seven
Signal Fire

David got up at sunrise, stoked his fire and went out to check his box trap. Something had been in it and eating at the guts. It looked like maybe a fox or a coyote by the tracks. Whatever it was, it was too big to get caught under the coke box. The box had been tipped over and his bait was gone. He reset the trap and went to gather more wood for his fire. Twice during the morning, he saw small planes go over, although not directly over. One was to the east of him and one to the west. He had waved his arms, but he knew there was zero chance that they had seen him. Around lunch time he thought that he had faintly heard the sound of a ski-doo or maybe a chain saw. It seemed to be coming from the south east of his location, but he wasn't sure if he'd actually heard something. It could just be his imagination. He went in to boil up some bush tea. He heated up one portion of the leftover meat and ate it.

In the afternoon, David saw his owl down the trail. It took off toward the south east. He decided that as soon as it warmed up a bit, he was going to leave this camp, even if it was the end of him, he would walk until he found Pete's cabin. His best guess was that it was south-east of his present location.

One thing he could do, was maybe get a signal fire ready. He had not been able to find a big enough clearing to build an S.O.S. signal that someone in a plane might see. There were always jets going over several times a day, but that was of no use to him. He could get a good pile of wood stacked with kindling underneath and have green branches to the side. Once the fire was going good, he could throw on the green branches to make some big smoke. He would have to have the signal fire near the cabin so that he could light it from his fire in the airtight stove. Thinking this through, he felt there was little chance it would work. He would have to see the plane, go in and fetch a burning branch. Take it out and get his fire going. Probably wait a good 5 minutes before the flames were big enough to throw on the green branches. By that time the plane would likely be gone.

Well he had nothing to do and nothing to lose so he spent the afternoon getting the signal fire ready to go. It was worth a shot.

That evening he ate the last of his meat. He checked his only trap. Nothing in the box. No guts left for bait either. He shouldn't have put them in all at once. Some fox had a nice meal. He wished he had some wire to make a snare, then he may be able to get a rabbit or some squirrels. It was no use wishing, he had none. At night he could hear the odd mouse, but he couldn't catch them at night. They were getting smarter he thought, because he never saw any during the day anymore.

For the next two days, it was too cold to go any distance with his spear. He caught nothing in the trap. He never saw a bush chicken, a rabbit, nothing. The following day it warmed up a bit. There had been no planes going over. He was losing the survival game and he knew it. He made up his mind that no matter the outcome, he was going to leave the next morning and search for Pete's cabin. It was his only hope. They obviously weren't searching for him. He had no idea why they weren't. It was a mystery to him. He was desperate to find food, so he had to strike out even if it meant dying on the trail. He would take one bottle of water and he had a glass pickle jar that he was going to put hot embers into. He didn't know if it would work, but he thought maybe he could start a fire with it if he had to. He would take the spear and his sleeping bag, but nothing else except the water bottle and the embers jar. He didn't want too much to carry. The spear he could use as a walking stick if nothing else. At daybreak tomorrow, he was leaving.

Chapter Twenty-Eight
Delusional

It was Dec 10th, one month since David had left. Harley and Janice were worried about Lorenda. They had tried calling a few times and there was no answer. The next morning, they drove over and rang the doorbell. They waited for quite some time before the front door opened.

"Mom, what's happened to your face. Do you have the flu or something? We tried calling several times yesterday and there was no answer. Where have you been?"

"Come in. I wasn't feeling well yesterday."

"Why is your face all red? Do you have the flu or something?"

"Don't worry, I'll be fine. It was just itchy for some reason."

Janice said " You should see a doctor, you don't look so good."

Lorenda had dark circles under her eyes and she smelled like a brewery, so she tried to keep her distance.

"I'm fine. Have you heard any news about your dad ? "

"No. I talked with Mike Kane yesterday. He said that he tried calling you as well. They would like to talk to you again. Perhaps you should call him."

"Did he say what he wanted?"

"No but I think you should call him."

"Does he have any new information?"

"Not that I know of."

Janice asked with apparent concern,

"Would you like to come stay with us for a couple days?"

"No, no, I'll be just fine. You guys go ahead with your day and I'll check in with you later."

"Well do you need anything? Anything we can get for you?"

"No nothing, really I'm fine. Thanks for looking in on me, but you guys get back to your day."

When Harley and Janice were back in their vehicle Janice blurted out

"Harley your mom's not doing too well." Did you see her face? What the hell is going on there?"

"I don't know, but whatever it is, it's not good. I'll check in with her more often. It looked like she was scratching her face or something."

"I know, she seemed very edgy. I guess that's not so unusual considering the circumstances."

"Well until we find dad, I guess we'll all be under a lot of stress."

Lorenda went over to the liquor cabinet and got out another bottle of gin. She poured herself a weak one and then called her boss at work. She explained to him about David's disappearance and told him that until further notice she couldn't come in to work. Her boss assured her that there was no problem. She would get her full wages under stress leave. He would drop off some paperwork in her mailbox that she would be required to fill out. If there was anything he could do to help, just call him.

Lorenda called her friend Cindy and asked if she could come over for a little visit. She needed someone to talk to.

That afternoon, they sat at Cindy's kitchen table.

"Lorenda, how are you doing? I've heard through the grapevine about David. What do you think happened? " "Make yourself comfortable dear. "Here, I'll pour us a drink."

"I really have no idea Cindy. David went off on an adventure into the bush up north. He was going to stay at a friends cabin. Harley and Rick went up there with the authorities, but there was no evidence or sign that he had ever been there. He just seemed to vanish."

"Lorenda, what are those red marks on your face? Do you have some kind of rash?" "Are you alright?"

Lorenda was wringing her hands.

"I must admit, I have been better. I'm beside myself with worrying about David."

"Yes, well I can imagine. You poor thing."

They sat talking for almost 2 hours in which time they finished off a bottle of wine and about a half bottle of gin.

Lorenda stopped at the liquor store on the way home and purchased another 4 bottles of gin.

When she got home she warmed up some leftover sausage and potatoes from the fridge. She had a glass of wine with her meal and then went upstairs and stared out the window. She locked the bedroom door. She watched every car go by. There were a couple vehicles that went by pretty slow. That was likely the police watching her house she surmised. She went downstairs and found a pair of binoculars. She checked and double checked that the back and front doors were locked. She closed all the blinds and curtains. Back in her bedroom upstairs, she once again locked the door. She studied every person walking on the street. She was looking for David. She had a gut feeling that he was watching her somehow. One of these days he would come for her. Tomorrow she would go buy a gun. She had to protect herself now.

Late that afternoon, detective Kane called again. She answered this time. He asked if he could come over. He had a few more questions. Lorenda put him off by telling him that she was ill. She would call him back when she was feeling better. Fuck that son of a bitch. He knew something was not right with her. Maybe David had talked to Kane and now they were plotting together to build a case against her. They no doubt, were going to try to prove attempted murder. They were setting her up. David must have taken the Excedrin, but it didn't kill him. She wondered if Harley and Rick were in on this too. It was all just too confusing. She would likely end up going to jail. She poured another gin.

Chapter Twenty-Nine
Making a break for it.

David woke up and stoked his fire. He was leaving this morning, come hell or high water. Once again, he never had a very good sleep, as he had trained himself to wake up every time he turned over. He didn't want that fire to go out. He went out and filled the water bottles. He would take one with him and leave the rest behind, in case he had to return for some reason. He checked his box trap. Nothing in there. He replaced the firewood in the cabin and broke up some small kindling to restart a fire, and placed it beside the stove. In the event that he had to return, he might somehow be able to start a fire. He had no matches and his lighters were out of fuel, but still he would prepare as best he could.

It seemed a bit warmer this morning. He was guessing -15 C. He prepared himself mentally. He decided against the pickle jar, or the coffee pot, filled with hot embers in it. Too awkward to carry and not likely to work anyway. He took a one litre pop bottle of water along. He took his sleeping bag, but not the waterproof bag. Nothing else, save his spear which would double as a walking stick. He wanted to travel light. He was not going to come back unless he absolutely had to. His plan was to follow the trail back to where it came to a T. This time he would turn left instead of right. That would take him in a more or less south easterly direction, which he guessed is where he had to be going.

The day was bright, the birds were singing. Although he was hungry and weak, David felt good about what he considered would be his last attempt at finding Pete's cabin or some cabin that might have food in it. He walked along at a slow but steady pace. It was tough sluggin because the snow was pretty deep in spots.

He reached the spot where the trail came to an end and intersected with another. He stopped for a much - needed rest. He had been walking for nearly 3 hours. He sat on a tree that had fallen over. Up ahead he saw an owl sitting in a tree. It headed off in the direction that he was going to be going in. Was it that same owl? Was it a sign? David took this as a good omen. A small plane flew almost directly overhead. David waved his arms frantically, but there was no sign that the pilot had seen him.

Of course, Murphy's law, he was miles away from his signal fire now. If he didn't have bad luck, he wouldn't have any luck at all.

He set off once again. It was early afternoon. In about a miles distance, he came upon another trail that went off to the right. This trail was a little wider and looked like it had been more travelled. His hopes lifted a little. Then he saw a rusted- out tin can hanging on a branch at about eye-level. It was a marker he thought. Someone had once hung it there as a trail sign, maybe to indicate the way back to a cabin. His heart started beating faster and he picked up his pace. Fifty feet ahead he saw the owl again. It seemed to be waiting for him. As he stumbled along, he began to see other signs. Trees that had fallen across the trail, cut out with a chain saw. Nothing recent but never the less signs of a more travelled path. Now here was a small pile of firewood stacked along the trail. Someone had cut it but never got back to pick it up. He could see it was several years old, but none the less, it was a great sign.

David was excited, his urge was to run. He stopped to calm himself. The depth of the snow and his weakened condition prevented him from moving quickly, but he moved forward as fast as he could. Soon he was actually sweating despite the cold. He knew he had to slow down and cool off or he would freeze up.

He must keep his composure. Stay calm. Another couple hundred yards and he saw an old forty -five - gallon drum just off to the side. Maybe an old gas barrel. He knew he was getting closer. He came to a fairly steep embankment. The trail went down it and up the other side. David recognized this raveen, or he thought he did. If he was right, he was in behind Pete's cabin, maybe only another half mile to a mile away. As he was rushing down the raveen, he started to slip. His foot caught under a tree going across the path and he lunged forward. He heard a sickening snapping noise and felt a sharp pain in his ankle. When he came to a stop, David knew his ankle was broken. The pain was excruciating. He lay there for several minutes and then crawled up so that he was above the tree that was pinning his ankle. He used his spear as a lever and lifted the tree slightly in order that he could pull out his foot. The pain was making him grimace and moan. Using his spear as a crutch, very slowly and with much care he hobbled down the slope and up the other side. Now he was sweating profusely. Once he was up the other side and a few more yards down the path, he spotted something shiny up in the trees. The sun was shining off something. It was the chimney on the cabin! Although his ankle hurt like hell, he was nearly wild with joy. He had found Pete's cabin.

The key was hanging right where it was supposed to be, under an eave on the left- hand side. He opened the door and peered inside. It was dirty, dusty, full of mice droppings and spider webs. To David it looked like the Ritz. He forced himself to go around the cabin and take off the " bear boards" covering the windows. It wasn't easy and very painful hopping around on one foot. He could see man tracks all over the yard. Someone had been here, maybe looking for him.

Once inside, the first thing he did was to look in the medicine cabinet for pain killers. There was a bottle of Tylenol in there and he took three of them. It was well- stocked with Iodine, aspirins, hand lotions, polysporin, bandages and lots more. He hobbled over to the wood cook stove. There was plenty of wood cut and stacked in the wood box. Even kindling ready to light the fire. David ripped up some pages from some old newspapers and magazines. He placed the paper in the firebox and put the kindling on top of that. He was really pleased to see the metal dispenser on the wall was full of wooden matches. He adjusted the air intake on the stove and the damper and then lit the fire. Thank you Jesus! He was going to have a warm sleep tonight on a real bed, with a real mattress. It was an overwhelming feeling of relief and joy. He had overcome his ordeal. He was going to survive. Yes, he had a broken ankle, but that would heal.

He looked around the cabin. It was really well stocked with tools, axes, hatchets. In a cupboard he found clean bedding, pillows, towels and pillow cases. There was a 22 rifle in the corner. A large drum was full of macaroni, pasta noodles, rice, canned vegetables and canned fruits. The drum had a top that you could seal with a metal ring. This kept out any animals or insects. He figured there was enough food here to last him a month. There were several kinds of traps and stretching boards for the furs. All the dishes and pots and pans etc. that you would normally find in a cabin were there. David was saved.

He didn't think he could make it down to the river with his ankle in this shape, but he could melt snow on the stove for drinking and wash water. He set about this task before it got dark. There was a coal oil lamp and plenty of fuel. The long nights would no longer be dark. He went to the trap door and looked into the root cellar. This was a place where he and Pete would leave any left- over liquor when they went back home. Sure enough, there was about 30 oz. of rum and maybe twenty of rye whiskey. He poured himself a nice drink of rum and sat by the stove enjoying the warmth that it was emitting. He never enjoyed a drink more. It made him light- headed immediately. There was plenty of wood in the cabin to last the night. He boiled some water in a pot and made some Kraft dinner. He ate the whole thing. Serving for four it said on the box. He stoked the fire and spread out his sleeping bag on the bed. He treated himself to another good shot of rum and another couple Tylenol to ease the pain in his ankle. He then, crawled into his sleeping bag and passed out. He was totally exhausted.

Chapter Thirty
Home sweet home

His ankle was throbbing when he woke up. It was 7 A.M. Still dark at this time of year. He hobbled over to the medicine chest and got himself 3 more Tylenol. Very little water left, but enough to have a good drink. He would have to get down to the river and chop a water hole in the ice, or if that proved to be too difficult, he would just melt snow in a tub on the stove. There was a large wash basin he could use, two five- gallon metal pails, or an actual round tub up in the loft that they used for bathing.

The cabin was 14ft wide and 20 ft long. A large trappers shack compared to most in that fur block. There was a loft, with wood stairs leading up to it from the middle of the room. The loft was 6 ft by 14 ft. It contained water barrels, an assortment of hand tools, a couple of old mattresses, a chain saw, some odds and ends of building materials and hardware, stretching boards for the furs, and rubber boots.

David had helped Pete build this cabin along with some of Pete's other friends and his brother Paul. It was made of logs, but the roof and floor were made with planks they had floated down the Beacon on a raft that they constructed from two canoes lashed together. It was a labor of love that took two summers to complete. David wasn't there all the time. He just came and helped when he could steal some time off from his business. They had brought in metal sheeting for the roof and fiberglass insulation to put beneath the floor. Windows were hauled in. It was everyone's first go at cabin building, so it wasn't perfect, but it was pretty darn good, and it was warm. Mosquitoes and horse flies plagued them constantly during the construction. They slept in tents and cooked on camp stoves and open fires. Hard work but a pile of fun too.

David used a corn broom as a crutch, and hobbled up the stairs to see what was all up there. He brought the tub down and put it on the stove. He went outside and got a 5 gallon pail full of snow and put it in the tub. He lit the fire and then found some dish soap. First on the agenda would be to wash out all the pails and the tub. He then would fill the tub with snow and begin to wash up the pots, pans, dishes etc. so that everything would be clean.

While the snow was melting, he took down a medicine box that hung on the wall. He found some elastic bandages and a couple of wood splints. He undressed and looked at his swollen ankle. He had no idea if he should try to set it or let it heal as is was. He sat on a chair and put his leg up on another chair. It looked fairly straight to him. He put the splints on either side of his foot, covering both sides of the ankle and wrapped it with the elastic bandages. He then put a wool sock over all of it. He would not be able to get a boot on, so he found a plastic bag and tied that over the sock. There would be no way he could get down to the river for a couple days, so snow melting would be the order of the day.

Time for breakfast. He rummaged through the store of food. There was quite a lot, yet he felt he should ration somewhat. This morning it would be a can of vegetable soup. He rinsed out a small pot, found the can opener and opened the tin. It smelled heavenly. He couldn't wait to taste the soup. He put it on the stove to heat. Real food, and the cabin was warming up nicely. He was just so happy. He had survived! The soup was absolutely delicious. When he finished, he wanted more, but he knew he shouldn't eat too much all at once. It would be a while before his stomach was back to normal. He hobbled outside and got two more pails of snow to melt. It seemed like he was in a different world. The memory of home, Lorenda and the boys seemed distant like someone else's life. It was so quiet here, still. There was no wind outside, he could hear the odd bird, but other than that nothing. After all the suffering in the past month, it felt like absolutely over the top fantastic to have a real roof over his head, food in the barrel, a warm place to rest and sleep. Security, at least for a while. He was overjoyed and so thankful. His ankle was throbbing. He took another two Tylenol. He wanted more whiskey, but he decided he would hold off on that until after he had his supper.

Over the next 3 hours, he melted snow and washed out cupboards, washed the knives and cutlery. Hobbling around he swept the floor, pulled down cobwebs from the corners and the stove pipes. He took stock as he went of all the treasures in the cabin. At lunch time, He cooked up a big pot of rice. He opened a can of tuna and mixed that in, added some soya sauce to the mixture and sat down for a feast. There was some orange pekoe tea for after the meal and then he stoked the wood stove and lay down for a sleep. He slept deeply.

It was after 2 when he woke up. He had to get more wood into the cabin. There was a wood -shed of sorts, not really a shed but a pole structure with a metal roof to keep the snow and rain off the wood. He figured the wood had been cut and split the last time Pete had been here. David guessed that was two, maybe three years ago. The wood was bone dry. Almost too dry. There was not enough sap in it, to burn with a lot of heat to it, but it was still okay. There was about a cord of wood put up. It would be enough to last a month before he would have to cut more. He didn't plan on being here more than that anyway. Once his ankle healed enough for him to walk on it, he would be out of here. Shouldn't be more than 3 weeks he figured. His food supply would be pretty much gone by that time anyway. He could hop around with a crutch but going out hunting was out of the question for the time being.

He could only carry two or three pieces of wood at a time because he had to use the crutch. This made for slow progress and to fill the wood box inside, it took about ten trips. One hour. A full wood box was enough to last 24 hours.

He loaded the 22 and set it by the door. You never know what might go through the yard. Maybe he would be lucky enough to get a deer or something. There was a radio on the window ledge, but the batteries were stone dead. He hoped he would come across some batteries but hadn't seen any yet. All the while during the afternoon, he melted more snow and filled the pails and tub. There was two bars of soap and a half dozen wash cloths. Tonight, he would have a good body wash and wash his hair. The dish soap bottle was only about a third full, so he would have to use it sparingly.

For the remainder of the afternoon, he fashioned a useable crutch from a stretcher board that was normally used to stretch a wolf skin. He had found a hand saw and cut a notch in the stretcher that would fit under his arm. He then wrapped that with a small cushion and fastened it all with duct tape. It was a huge improvement from the corn broom crutch.

He poured himself a rye and water and enjoyed a drink while he prepared a supper of Spaghetti and tomato sauce. There were only three 8 oz tins of the sauce, but he felt okay about using one up tonight as he felt like celebrating his good fortune. He put a pail of water on the stove to heat.

After eating, he stoked the fire and striped off his clothes. That was a bit of work, as he had to take off his splint to remove his pants and long johns. He washed himself from head to toe and then washed his hair in the basin using some of the dish soap. By the time, he dried and put his splint back on, it was fairly late. The coal oil lamp cast a warm glow. He could hear wolves howling in the distance. Was it the same wolf pack that he had seen? Probably. He hobbled outside to take a leak and was treated to a display of the northern lights. Except for the pain in his ankle, he almost felt like he was on a vacation now. He took another two Tylenol and poured himself about 4 oz of rum. He put his injured leg up on a chair and he read a trapper's magazine while he drank. Then stoked the airtight stove. He set the air intake to just a crack, so that it would burn most of the night and crawled into a warm bed. He was in heaven. He remembered all those nights in the bush freezing and fighting to keep warm. The booze and the Tylenol eased the pain in his ankle, and he slept like a log.

Chapter Thirty-One
Kane investigates

Over the past few days, Lorenda stayed pretty much sedated with gin. She only left the house once to go for some groceries and toilet paper. It had snowed a bit, but she never bothered to shovel the walk. She only answered the phone when the kids called. They knew there was something terribly wrong with Lorenda, but she kept them at bay. She spent long hours watching through the windows at people and traffic passing by. Lorenda was sure the house was being watched. She was almost out of Gin again but didn't want to leave the house, so she called a dial a bottle service to bring her four more bottles of Gin.

The hours went by slowly. Her mind went through every scenario. What had happened to David? Why was there no trace of him? He somehow must have discovered the cyanide and was now plotting his revenge against her. She prayed to God. If she could ever get out of this mess, she would never do anything bad again. She would rekindle her relationship with David and be a good wife to him for the rest of their lives. She stared through the binoculars at every person that walked by on the street. None of them were David, but she thought many looked like they may be undercover police, just watching her house.

Harley called her. He said he was worried about her and was coming over. She couldn't change his mind, so she relented. Could he wait for an hour or two? She had to have a little time to clean up and put away the gin bottles.

Harley and Janice came together. Lorenda had done her hair a bit and put on some makeup.

Janice looked pitifully at Lorenda and asked, "What are all these little scabs on your face and arms mom?" "Have you developed some kind of skin condition?"

Lorenda looked away.

"It's nothing. My skin is dry, and I find it itchy, so I scratch it." "I guess I'm nervous and upset that we can't find David."

Harley came over and put his arm around his mother's shoulder.

"Mom you look terrible, there are dark circles under your eyes. Are you not sleeping well?"

"Of course, I'm not. I'm worried about your father. Don't tell me you're not losing sleep over it."

"Well to be honest, I guess we all are. You've got to try to take care of yourself mom or you're going to make yourself sick. Is there anything we can do for you?"

"Well yes there is. I'll make a list and maybe you could bring me some groceries. I really don't feel like going out."

She made them a cup of tea. The conversation was strained

They talked about David and about the police and how they weren't making any headway in finding out what may have happened to David. Lorenda promised to call Janice everyday and let them know if she needed anything. They felt there was nothing more that they could do to locate David. Either the police would find him, or he would just show up one day and solve the mystery.

Two minutes after they left, Lorenda poured herself a stiff one. She made sure the doors were locked and closed all the blinds. She went upstairs to her bedroom and stared out the window to the street below. There was a young couple walking by, arm in arm. They looked like they were talking and laughing. They glanced toward her house and carried on. Good acting

Lorenda thought. They were watching her. They certainly looked suspicious. Yes, her house was being watched. They couldn't fool her. An hour later, she was passed out. The bottle was three quarters empty.

Detective Kane didn't know why Lorenda was avoiding him, but it made him suspicious of her. She was keeping something from him. He felt she had some part in David's disappearance. He had to question her again. Even though he had no real evidence against her, he knew it's more often the spouse that's responsible. He was going to nail her if she was responsible. Something would break in this case. It was a matter of time. He was beginning to think that maybe, just maybe, David had not run off. Maybe he was no longer alive. David had left on Nov 10th. That was over a month ago. There were no phone calls, only one credit card transaction in Lovely on the same day that he left. That would indicate he was headed toward his friends cabin as he had planned. In spite of being in Lovely on Nov 10th, there was absolutely no sign that he had made it to the cabin. So where did he go from Lovely? Not a trace after that. How can you make a vehicle disappear? Lorenda hadn't been with him, so in what way was she connected? It was a real puzzler. He had to admit he was at a dead end. He would interview more people from Smiths Lock and Key to see if he could turn up any new clues.

Chapter Thirty-Two
Nightmare

David's dream was that he was out in the bush and didn't know which way to turn. It was brutally cold, and he was freezing. Every minute felt like an hour. He woke up in a sweat. He got up and made some tea. His ankle felt a little better. He took two Tylenol for the pain. After a breakfast of kraft diner, he wrapped his foot with a blanket and tied it on good. He put the wrapped foot into a couple plastic bags to keep it dry and then dressed warmly to go out and bring in snow for melting and to gather wood from the pile. He was going to bring in a lot of wood and split it. The dream of freezing was preying on his mind. He never wanted to spend another cold night in his life. His experience of sleeping out in the woods had traumatized him. All through the morning and until mid - afternoon, he hauled in wood. He made a pile against the wall maybe 5 times more than he needed for one day. It exhausted him. He then made himself a stiff drink and sat at the table with a pencil and a sheet of blank paper. He began to plan how long it would take him to walk out to safety and what he would take with him. He made a list, just as he had when he left home. It would be a good long walk. At least 36 miles to get out to the main road.

He poured a second rum, mixed it with some water. He ran his hands through his hair, and he rubbed his head. He really needed a haircut. His thoughts drifted to his ordeal and all the hardship that brought him here. The experience had a purpose he felt. It had softened his feelings towards Lorenda. He knew he hadn't been a great dad to his boys and the grandkids. David resolved to spend more quality time with them when he got back home. He would make amends with Lorenda and take her on a holiday. Everyone at Smith's Lock and Key was going to get a raise. He would be more generous, and he was going to start spending some of the money they had accumulated.

He went up to the loft to take stock of what was all up there. In one of the pails, he found a dozen D batteries. Those would fit in the radio downstairs. He was anxious to see if any of them had any juice left in them. Coming down, on the second step he tripped and fell down to the floor, banging his head on the airtight stove. There was no railing along the steps. He had fallen about seven feet, straight down. Blackness.

When he came to, there was a pool of blood around his head. It was dark, and the fire was out. His left wrist and arm throbbed. Extreme pain. His nose was cut, as well as his eyebrow. He couldn't see much out of his left eye. He slowly got to his knees and then his feet. He hobbled over to the table with much difficulty and lit the lamp. He sat on the edge of the bed nearly blacking out from the pain in his arm and wrist. He sat there for about five to ten minutes. He really had no concept of time. He slowly got up and opened the medicine cabinet. He took out three Tylenol and then got the rum bottle and washed them down. He sat down, and in another minute, he passed out again.

When he finally regained consciousness, it was still dark. He didn't know if an hour passed or maybe it was a day. Once again, he had woken up on the floor. He must have fallen off the chair when he passed out. His wrist and arm were causing him a lot of pain. As if in slow motion he prepared the kindling and lit a fire. The lamp was still burning so he couldn't have been unconscious for too long. There was blood all over his face and it had run down his neck and soaked the upper part of his shirt. What a colossal mistake. Such an innocent thing had caused so much damage. He found he couldn't think clearly. His head hurt; he was dizzy. David took a good slug of rum, hoping to kill the pain. He filled the fire box in the stove as much as possible and crawled into his sleeping bag, trying to favor his broken arm and wrist. Blackness.

Outside the tree- tops swayed in the breeze. A light snow was falling. The forest was silent and still. From somewhere there came the hoot of an owl.

Chapter Thirty-Three
Tragedy

Back at home, Lorenda turned over in her bed. It was the middle of the night and she was wide awake. She remembered when she had first met David, how much in love she had been. What had happened to her? She tried to think of what made them pull apart. What was so wrong that they now hated each other? It seemed like a lifetime away, as if she was watching a movie about two other people. She got out of bed and put on her housecoat. She still had her clothes on, but that didn't really matter to her. She made her way downstairs and rummaged through the fridge for something to eat. There was some cheese and sausage which she wolfed down and then got a bottle of gin and made herself a large drink. She positioned a chair at the front window in the living room and sat looking out at the street. The curtains spread just enough for her to peep out. She sat sipping on the gin and staring out. The street was empty, but she sensed that someone was watching the house. It was very frightening. It made her nervous as a cat on a hot tinned roof. She scratched at her face. There was some movement in a pine tree in the front yard. It was a large bird of some type. It looked like an owl. That was weird. She had never seen an owl in the yard before. Not even in the neighborhood. In fact, she had never even seen an owl other than in a zoo. A car drove by slowly. It looked like they were watching the house. They were definitely on to her. She thought of David. What had happened to him? Where was he? He must have figured out that she had tried to kill him. Another car went slowly by. It wasn't the same car and it looked like maybe an Asian girl driving it. In about 20 minutes she went to refill her glass. She went upstairs and locked her door. She sat sipping and staring out the window. After she finished the gin, she crawled back into bed and slept fitfully. She dreamed that David came to the foot of her bed. He looked down at her with disgust. He had something in his hand that she could not make out. Was it a gun? She jumped up with a start. She was wet with perspiration. Lorenda was scared stiff. The room was dark and cold. She got up and ran to the window. It was quiet outside, no movement anywhere. She went and checked the lock on the door. It was still locked. She had the heebie jeebies. She was sweating and felt like throwing up. She had another sip of the gin and then rushed to the toilet and vomited.

The next afternoon, Rick and Mattie went over to Lorendas. They had tried calling her several times that morning, but there was no answer. Rick unlocked the front door with his key and called in

"Mom, it's Rick and Mattie. Mom, mom are you here?" Only silence met them. They slowly made their way around the main floor calling out. Then they went upstairs and looked around. Lorenda's bedroom door was locked. They knocked on the door and called her name. Only silence. Rick didn't have a key for the door, so he put his shoulder to it. It wouldn't give in.

"Mattie, I'll go downstairs and find some tools or a sledge-hammer. You keep trying to wake her. Rick ran down the stairs and Mattie continued to bang on the door calling out for her mother- in- law.

Rick found a sledgehammer and brought it upstairs. Mattie backed out of the way and Rick swung in a wide arc hitting the door handle. The door banged open. They found Lorenda on the bed. She was fully clothed and had a house coat on over the clothes. She smelled awful and they could see stains from the vomit down her front. They shook her and patted her face.

"Mom wake up! Mom, Mom."

There was no movement. She felt cold to the touch.

"Mattie, call 911! Hurry. They looked around the room and saw an empty bottle of Gin on top the dresser. There was a Tylenol bottle on the bedside table with the cap off and a few capsules spilled onto the tabletop. A glass of gin lay spilt on the tabletop as well.

The paramedics arrived in a few minutes. They tried to revive her, but she was gone. The paramedics called a coroner, and then sat talking quietly, waiting for his arrival. Rick and Mattie were crying and making phone calls to Harley and Janice, to her parents and other family members. The coroner, an elderly man with white hair and a mustache arrived in about forty minutes. He was dressed in a loose, ill-fitting suit and wore a fedora hat. His round glasses made him look the part of a coroner. He examined the body, pronounced Lorenda dead and filled out the necessary paperwork, making notes about the gin bottle and the Tylenol capsules. He explained because she had died at home, an autopsy had to be performed. The next day, when that was done; the cause of death was found to be cyanide poisoning. Although a thorough investigation was carried out, there was no cyanide found in the house.

Detective Kane and others found this to be very strange. He wondered if this could have been a suicide or were the children involved in some way. He knew from previous investigations that Harley had a gambling problem and was seriously in debt. Rick and Mattie were not doing well financially either. They both would be questioned. With their father missing and their mother dead, they stood to get the inheritance. His gut instinct told him, Harley and Rick were involved.

Chapter Thirty-Four
Discovery

Nick and Sadie had gotten up early. They ate a huge breakfast of porridge, toast and fruit. They had just bought two new Polaris 1100 snowmobiles the previous week and today they would be making their first big trip with them. They packed a lunch and all the necessities to make a fine wiener roast in the woods. Two thermoses full of hot chocolate would keep them warm. Along with the new snow machines, they had purchased new snowmobile suits and heated helmets. They were decked out and anxious to get out to the winter wilderness. The route planned took them down the Beacon river and would follow it until about 1PM when they would have lunch. After that they would turn around and make their way back to their truck and trailer, so they could load up before dark.

There was lots of fresh powdery snow and it was a great sunny day. Perfect temperature for sleddin. -12 Celsius. The middle-aged couple were thoroughly enjoying their adventure. At 12:30 Nick stopped in the middle of the river. This was a good spot to have lunch. They sat on the seats of the sleds, eating sandwiches and drinking coco. Nick had brought a small bottle of Irish cream to put into the hot chocolate, to celebrate their inaugural run. They had decided against the wiener roast as it might make them later than they wanted before they turned around. They were having a wonderful time.

Sadie noticed the sun glinting off something high up the bank. It aroused their curiosity and they studied it for several minutes while they ate and discussed what it might be. It was something shinny. Nick thought it must be a piece of tin or something. He

then noticed a small opening through the brush on the bank. When they were done eating and had packed away the thermoses, they walked over and discovered it was a trail going up. Sadie said,
"We have time, lets walk up and see what it is."
Nick agreed and they set off. They were startled about half-way up when an owl took flight from a pine tree directly in front of them.
"Holy, that scared the shit out of me." Sadie exclaimed.
They made their way up and came to a clearing with a log cabin sitting in the centre of it. There were no tracks in the yard. There was no smoke coming from the chimney. Nick was kind of excited.
"Let's have a look inside. Looks like a hunters cabin".
Sadie was a bit nervous.
"Let's not. That's trespassing". "Look the windows are not boarded up, so someone must be coming and going" she said.
"If no one was using this place they would have the bear boards on."
Nick said, "Oh come on, there's no one around, there's no fresh tracks around here."
Sadie followed behind him. Nick went to the door and scraped some snow away with his boot. The door was kind of frozen shut, so he had to give it a good hit with his shoulder and it burst open. Although the windows were not boarded up, it was dim inside. There was a putrid smell that filled their nostrils immediately. They stepped back and let their eyes adjust.
"What the hell is that smell?" asked Nick. Sadie was very nervous.
"Let's get out of here."
Nick wrapped his arms around her and held her to calm her down.
"You stay out here. I'm going in to look around."
He put his scarf up over his nose to try to protect himself from the smell. He went in slowly and the first thing he noticed

was that there was an awful lot of wood stacked inside the cabin. That was unusual. There were packages of food out on the table and a bottle of whiskey, almost empty. It looked like there was someone or something in the bed.

"Hello, hello."

He went forward slowly and pulled back the covers. There was a body there. He thought it looked like a man. He quickly replaced the covers over the mans head and rushed out of the cabin. Sadie saw the panic in his face as he emerged into the light.

"What's wrong?"

Nick ran a couple steps passed her.

"There's a dead body in there! Will our cell phones work here? See if you have a signal."

Sadie checked her cell phone. No service. She tried 911 anyway. No go. Nick was really shaken. "Let's close that door and get back to the sleds."

They left in a hurry and called 911 when they were back out on the highway. They gave the police their story and directions on how to get to the cabin. Later that day, the body was identified as David Smith. Rick and Harley were notified. The body was well preserved because of the cold. When they got it to Prescott, an autopsy showed the cause of death to be a brain bleed due to blunt trauma to the head.

Detective Kane was also notified, and along with the local police, he made a trip out to the scene. Initially they thought there might be foul play due to the injuries and bruises to the body, but they ruled that out. David's broken ankle had been bandaged and because there was a pool of blood soaked into the floor beside the airtight stove, they were able to put two and two together and deduced he had fallen from the loft.

David had his survival challenge and he had lost.

Lorendas gamble that she could do away with David without being caught was a success, or was it?

CPSIA information can be obtained
at www.ICGtesting.com
Printed in the USA
JSHW080805170323
39062JS00001B/3